I0784715

COLLEEN SNYDER

The Master's Keepers Series BondKeeper

Colleen Snyder

ISBN:978-1-968792-03-9

A NOTE FROM THE AUTHOR

A word about capital letters:

For those who serve the Master (the Lord Jesus), all pronouns are capitalized: He, His, Him, Whose, Who, etc.

For those who do NOT serve the Master, all pronouns are in lower case: he, his, him, whose, who etc.

My apologies to CMOS (The Chicago Manual of Style).

colleen snyder

CHAPTER ONE

Gentry's mother called from the living area, "Gentry, child, what are you doing in there? Come help me move the stew pot to the table. Wilma and Brody Swansworth are joining us tonight." The fifteen-year-old came in from her sleeping area off the side of the wooden cabin. She would have to warn Canna. The pearl dragon would need to hide deep in her cave along the river. Gentry would signal so the dragon knew not to approach the cabin. Only Gentry knew the dragon remained in the area. Even her parents believed Canna was gone, banished from the village and the surrounding forests.

Mother had the blackened kettle with its dinner of rabbit stew bubbling over the fire in the fireplace. It took both Mother and Gentry to safely lift the heavy-laden cauldron to the table. They set it on a stone platter to keep it from burning the wooden table beneath. Gentry arranged the benches along the sides and set the earthenware bowls with metal forks and spoons alongside each. Mother shook her head. "Go fetch the two extra settings."

Gentry ground her teeth in frustration. Wilma only wanted one thing: for Gentry to be pledged in marriage to Brody. Brody only wanted one thing: to eat Mother's cooking. No older than Gentry herself, Brody loved to eat. He especially loved Mother's food. Gentry and her family were once invited to a meal at Wilma's. Though the widow was far richer than Gentry's family, she set a meager table. Gentry was insulted for her mother, who always made the Cummings' family meals stretch for any visitor. But Wilma served only what she must and complained about the effort.

Mother rushed past Gentry. "You look preoccupied, child. What are you thinking about?" It was clear the preparations for dinner concerned Mother.

Gentry didn't want to admit she was brooding about Wilma and her rudeness. She said, "I miss Canna." Mother stopped to stroke her daughter's deep red hair. "I'm sorry you had to send her away. I know you loved the dragon. But the villagers—"

Gentry finished her mother's statement. "— were frightened of her. And blamed her for every lost sheep and every missing child. Canna would never hurt a human. And she never stole anyone's animals. Those were lies Francis Miller told. No children in this village ever disappeared. None."

She hadn't intended to bring up the past. But tears sprung into her eyes. Her voice reflected her bitterness. "Francis Miller hates anything he can't control. And no one controls Canna. That's why he tried to have her killed. They hunted her until she had to leave." Gentry's tears fell freely. "She's alone. She has no one to talk to. I promised I'd always take care of her." She looked at her mother. "You promised you'd help me."

"I can't stop people being afraid of her. She's bigger than the house."

"Is that her fault? Dragons grow. People are only afraid of her because Francis Miller made nasty lies about her stealing his sheep."

"Must we have this discussion again? Francis Miller swore he saw Canna snatch one of his lambs. He said she'd eaten five others."

Gentry wanted to stomp her feet but respected her mother too much. Still, she would not let the matter drop. "Canna brought back one of the missing lambs as evidence she hadn't taken them. Francis Miller swore it wasn't his. He said she must have stolen it from some other farmer and pretended it was his. As if Canna would lie. She follows the Master. She wouldn't lie."

Mother sighed. "I know, child. Your father paid

him back for the missing lambs. It hurt, but the flock multiplied with a good lambing. Now, Wilma and Brody will be here soon. Let's have no more talk of Canna tonight. She's gone now, and we can't bring her back. She's away somewhere safe. She'll be fine on her own. Dry your face."

Gentry did as Mother told her. She slipped outside and ran to the back of the small property they called home. The girl shimmied up the pine tree and hung her red scarf from the highest limb. Canna would see it and know to hide deep in the caves. Canna and Gentry had started using the signal before the dragon was exiled.

Gentry remembered their conversation.

"It's not right, and it's not fair!" Gentry stormed.

Canna nodded her huge pearlescent head. "Agreed. But hiding in the caves is the only way for me to stay safe. With the men out hunting me, I can't come near you."

Gentry's eyes narrowed, then widened. "I have an idea. I'll put up a signal. I'll…I'll put a scarf in the tree. If it's red, you'll know to go to the back of the caves. If it's white, it's safe to meet me at the river."

"What if someone sees the scarf? What will you tell them?"

"I'm signaling a friend over the hill. They won't ask who. Lots of people do it." Gentry grinned. "It's perfect. You'll be safe, and we can keep meeting."

And it worked, too. For now. Until Canna and Gentry could figure out what to do. It was getting dangerous for Canna to merely hide in the caves.

Francis Miller didn't believe Canna was gone. He threatened to use Gentry to find the dragon. He confronted Father at the mill and swore Canna was still in the area, still stealing sheep. Worse, he tried to convince people Canna had killed a child, and more than likely ate him. A boy was missing, anyhow, from over in Lughton, the village farthest from the river and hardest to get to. No one was willing to take the three days needed to walk there and back to prove Mister Miller's claims. Gentry swore she would, but Father said no one would believe her if she did go. And he couldn't take the time away from planting. No, Canna would have to fend for herself. Best she was gone, whether Francis Miller believed it or not.

Gentry came back into the house before Wilma and Brody arrived. The girl knew the two would be late. They always were. The disrespect for her mother made Gentry angry, but Mother said it didn't matter. Wilma Swansworth was the richest person in the village and used her wealth to get what she wanted. And what she wanted was Gentry to marry Brody.

Brody was spoiled, rude, and not to be trusted. Jansen, however, another boy Gentry's age, was not only fine to look at, but also had a pleasant manner that won hearts of mothers—and fathers. Hard working, honest. If Gentry were looking for a husband, Jansen would be a prize.

But she wasn't looking. Gentry cleaned her tunic. She thought about leaving it dirty but didn't want to insult her mother. Canna often reminded Gentry to respect her parents. While she had them. They were a blessing Canna never knew. No, Canna was alone in the world.

The dragon often went on trips to find others of her kind. She might be gone a week, sometimes two, on occasion. The longest she'd been away was a month. She never spoke of what she did or where she'd been. But the last of the reports was the same. "No, I didn't find anyone around here. They've all gone over the mountains." Always over the mountains.

Wilma Swansworth limped to the cabin on her son Brody's arm. She sighed deeply as she crossed the threshold into the house. "When did the distance between our houses get so much further? I don't know how many more times I can make these trips." The silver-haired woman wore a long blue robe over her floor-length dress. It made her look like the royalty she claimed to be. Though few believed her, no one challenged her. It wasn't polite, Mother said.

Gentry clenched her jaws. She'd seen Wilma around the market. The woman didn't limp at the time. Only when someone watched. But the girl kept her observations to herself. Mother had been with her when she saw Wilma waltz around a new wagon she bought. Mother knew. If Mother stayed silent, Gentry would as well.

Father helped the older woman to the table and a seat on the bench. Brody dropped into the chair at the head of the table in Father's usual place. He smiled at Gentry, and his eyes glinted. "Nice to be invited, finally."

Mother managed a proper smile. "Yes, it is good to have you here."

Wilma gave another great sigh. "It will be much easier when Brody and Gentry are wed. They can purchase my little cottage on the river. It sits halfway between our two properties. Then neither of us will have to go far to visit."

Mother cleared her throat. "*If* the children marry, Wilma. No one has made a pledge yet."

Wilma shrugged. "Such details. Brody is ready to ask for her hand, aren't you, Brody?"

Brody frowned. "No."

Wilma laughed. "He jokes. Of course he is." The woman glared at her son. He ignored her.

Mother hesitated, but said, "Why don't we eat while the stew and the biscuits are hot?"

Wilma sniffed. "Stew again? Oh, well. Your stew is excellent. What is it this time? Lamb?"

Father took a place at the foot of the table, usually reserved for Mother. Mother sat beside

Gentry, opposite Wilma. Father motioned to the pot. "Rabbit. Mother makes the best rabbit stew in all of Gander."

Wilma shrieked, "Rabbit?"

Mother's cheeks reddened, and she lowered her eyes. Gentry's insides burned. Father said evenly, "Yes, rabbit. The Master provided them for us to eat, and we are grateful for His provision."

Wilma raised her eyebrows. "You have a flock of sheep as well."

Father said quickly, "That are lambing, and the lambs must stay with their dams for at least seven days, or the health of the mother suffers. You will love the stew. I guarantee it."

Brody tapped his foot. "Can we get on to the eating?"

Mother lifted her eyes. "Father, will you say the blessing?"

Brody gave an exaggerated sigh, but Father bowed his head and folded his hands. Gentry did the same. Father intoned, "We come before You as obedient sheep. Bless this nourishment You have given. Bless this time, bless our guests, and bless this home. In Your Name we pray, amen."

Brody grabbed a biscuit off the platter. He crammed it in his mouth and grabbed a second one before the plate passed to his mother. She only smiled at him, took one of the buttery pillows, then passed them to Father. Father took one, passed the plate to Mother, who handed the platter to Gentry without taking any. Gentry followed her mother's lead. Save them for the guests.

Father ladled out the stew. Wilma eyed it with suspicion but sampled it. Her eyes widened, and she glared at Father. "You said this was rabbit."

"It is. I caught them yesterday."

"It tastes exactly like beef. Surely you are joking."

Father shook his head. "No, I'm not. We don't keep cattle. Only sheep and goats. I saw the rabbits in the garden and thought I would try to snare them. I didn't believe I would catch them. But I caught two." He chuckled.

Wilma sniffed. But she ate what was in her bowl. And asked for more.

Brody ate three helpings. Gentry made sure to only take a small ladle full. She would not allow her mother to be embarrassed by running out of food. Especially with Wilma and Brody as guests.

Dinner progressed without conversation and was soon over. Gentry cleared the table of bowls and utensils. Mother brought out the walnut pie she baked earlier in the day. She divided it into six equal pieces. Gentry knew the sixth piece would be for Father's lunch tomorrow.

Brody took two pieces. As did his mother. Father took one piece. Mother looked at the pie plate and passed it to Gentry. "Here, dear. I'm not hungry."

Gentry set the plate down without taking the pie. "I'm full as well. We'll save the last piece for father for later."

Brody shoveled his pie into his mouth, grabbed the pie tin, and slid the remaining cut of pie onto his plate. He grinned wide and stuck his fork into the walnut confection. Wilma smiled at Mother. "Thank you for the delicious pie. It's obvious Brody loves it. You must be sure to teach Gentry how to prepare it." She stopped, arched her eyebrows, and asked, "She can cook, of course?"

Mother nodded. "Of course. She watches me cook most days."

Wilma frowned. "Watching and doing are very different. Brody requires a wife who can satisfy his stomach's needs. Perhaps you should allow Gentry to prepare the meals for the remainder of the time before the wedding. I'm sure she would be happy to take the burden off your hands."

Mother looked at her hands. "Cooking is never a burden for me. And there is no wedding planned as of yet. Gentry has her own concerns."

Brody sneered, "Yeah, like playing with that hideous dragon the past few years. Good thing Francis Miller saw its true colors. Who knows how long it would continue to terrorize our village?"

Gentry's face burned. Her hands shook. She clenched her teeth, ready to bark her answer. But

Mother put her hand on Gentry's arm and squeezed it in warning. Gentry breathed out slowly.

Father shrugged. "The dragon is long gone. We saw her leave. She will not bother this village anymore. Gentry has duties in the field with me. Since I don't have a strapping son like you do, Wilma, Gentry must carry the load of learning both her mother's role and mine. When she marries, she'll be a well-suited helpmate to whoever her husband may be." Father stressed the words, *when* and *may*. He held Gentry's eyes.

Gentry lowered her head. Father would protect her. Father would never force her to marry Brody. No matter what Wilma Swansworth said.

Wilma cleared her throat. "Yes, well, I'm sure you'll be able to find other help once Brody and Gentry wed. She'll need to attend to Brody full time." Wilma patted her son's arm. "He has many needs."

Father said firmly, "*If* the children wed, it will be at a time of their choosing. My daughter has yet to indicate whether she is even ready for a husband, much less who that might be. They both have time. Let them grow."

Wilma leaned forward, and her eyes narrowed. "I am not a well woman. I'm afraid my time on this earth grows ever shorter. I will see my son wed. Gentry is the only young woman of age to marry. She's perfect for him."

Brody snorted. "Except for the dragon affair."

Mother squeezed Gentry's arm again. Gentry held her tongue.

Wilma shrugged. "The affair has been settled. The dragon is gone. Gentry knows better than to mention the beast again." She stared hard at Gentry. Gentry held the woman's eyes even with her own. She would give Wilma Swansworth nothing.

Wilma dropped her eyes. "I want the children wed by midsummer. That gives you one planting season to finish your labors in the field. Then she will marry Brody and start tending to her new family duties."

Mother spoke. "It's too soon. And Gentry hasn't said she wants to marry Brody."

Wilma waved her hand as if it were nothing. "A proper child will do what her parents command. If you're worried about losing her help, I will pay for an assistant for the fields." She looked at Father. "You'll get twice the work from a man than you will from your daughter. Think of the crops you will plant. If that's not enough, I can pay to double your flock of sheep."

Gentry's eyes widened. Was Wilma trying to buy her as a wife for Brody?

What would more help and more sheep mean to Father and Mother? Security in their old age? More money? Less work? Would it really tempt Father? Would he really give her up?

Father shook his head. "My daughter is not for sale. If she chooses to wed, that is her concern. The matter is closed."

Wilma stood. "The matter is closed, certainly." Fire flared in her eyes. Her voice hardened. "Gentry and Brody will marry, and by midsummer. I will see to it. And you know I get my way." She looked at her son. "Come along, Brody. We're done here."

The two left without a thank you for the meal or the invite. Wilma swept out the door, her son in tow.

Father waited until Wilma was gone, stood, and closed the door. Mother seethed beside Gentry. "That woman. That terrible woman. Coming to our house and telling us what we will do? How dare she?"

Father leaned against the doorpost. "She dares, because no one tells her no. She gets her way because people are afraid to stand against her. And she has too many who will do her bidding and be happy of it."

Gentry stared at the floor. What Father said was true. Wilma did get her way. Always. But not this time. Gentry would not wed Brody Swansworth, no matter what. Wilma would make life miserable for her parents, Gentry knew. She had ways to buy people's homes from under them, turning them out so she could build a larger shop or bigger barns. Always for the good of the village, of course. Progress. Wilma had the means to do whatever she wanted.

But she would not force Gentry to marry Brody. Gentry would run away first. If she were gone, Mother and Father would be safe from Wilma. Gentry and Canna would live down by the river. They would disappear. Tonight. Together.

* * *

CHAPTER TWO

Gentry cleaned the kitchen and banked the fire for the morning. She kissed her parents goodnight and slipped to her sleeping area. She stuffed clothes, food, and her most precious items in her backpack. Items like her favorite rock. The one she'd seen the morning she first found Canna at the creek. She wrapped into her tunic the bracelet her mother had tied around her wrist on Gentry's tenth birthday. The strings had become too worn to stay fastened, so Gentry kept the bracelet in a small pouch under her pillow. The young woman also packed the wooden flute her father carved for her last year. It might not be much use on the trip, but it would remind Gentry of her parents. Last of all was the dragon's harness, fashioned from Canna's instructions. It helped Gentry stay on during the flights the girl and dragon made. Before Francis Miller began his lies.

Gentry couldn't tell Mother or Father about her

plans. They would understand why she left, but no one would be able to force them to say where she had gone. They wouldn't know. And everyone believed Canna had already left the area. Only Francis Miller still swore Canna remained near the village. He hadn't seen her, of course. Canna was too careful. No, Francis Miller only wanted to scare folks into thinking Canna was stealing sheep. Gentry was half convinced the man was stealing them himself. She had no proof, but she suspected he was capable.

She waited until she heard her father's snores and her mother's high-pitched whistles to slip out the back door. She wrapped her dark green cloak over her pack, pulled her hood over her head, and made her way to the river. Gentry walked without making a sound. Her kidskin boots cushioned the pine needles beneath her feet. Canna had trained her well in moving unheard through the brush. Stealth served Gentry well on her trips to spend time with the dragon. Many the time she avoided a hunter or trapper looking for game for his family…or searching for Canna.

Not that the dragon was easy to find. Canna could blend in with the trees and brush if she chose. She hid best submerged in the river. Her white scales shimmered in the depths. Beautiful to behold, the sight was always mistaken as sun on the water.

Gentry froze. Voices drifted across the distance. Close, but not too.

"I know I saw the dragon. I will kill it. Stealing my sheep. Mine. Always mine."

Francis Miller. Gentry's hackles rose. But she stayed silent, unmoving.

Another voice, harsh in its delivery, answered back. "Save your lies for someone else. I've seen the flock you keep hidden in the vale. You blame the dragon for stealing yours, and Farmer Cummings gives you one of his sheep to make up for it. Now you have two flocks. Your trick may work on the farmer, but not on me. I'm here for the reward."

Gentry's eyes widened. Reward?

"Dragon teeth. Every one worth a mint. Over in Callig, they pay handsomely for all of them. Grind 'em up, use the powder for healing potions or some such rot. I don't care, so long as they buy them. You can claim all the glory you want for being the savior of your village. I want the teeth."

Gentry covered her mouth and drew in a deep breath. Canna would have to leave —now. The girl had only thought of the two of them living by the river. Now, they needed to flee. Forever.

The men walked off, still talking. "If the thing is anywhere, it's in the caves."

"I count fifty caverns big enough to hide the monster. If we had the girl, we could force the dragon out of hiding," Francis Miller sneered.

The second voice, the one after Canna's teeth, was sharp in reply. "I live among these people. I would not be able to face her parents if she were killed."

Miller snorted. "Why should we care? The dragon killed her. That's all anyone needs know."

"No one will believe the dragon would kill its master. Gentry Cummings raised it from a lizard. The two are bonded. A dragon would die before injuring its bond-mate."

"How do you know so much about dragons, Trelove?"

"I have traveled." The mystery man said no more.

Gentry had no time to wonder who Trelove might be. She'd not heard the name before. It didn't matter. All that mattered was reaching Canna to warn her.

The men followed the easiest route to the river, but not the quickest. Gentry could cut across the cliffs and climb down from above. But at night? Alone? She had counted on her many trips to the caves to take her safely there this evening. She could follow the path with her eyes closed. But the trip over the ravine could be treacherous. Rock falls and slides were many and too easily stumbled upon in the dark. As frustrating as it was, she would have to follow the men and hope they didn't find Canna at the first cave they came to.

Why did she have no way to warn Canna? She had heard lore of people speaking to dragons with their mind. But if Canna had the ability, she had never shared it with Gentry.

It didn't mean Gentry wouldn't try. She closed her eyes and thought as hard as she could. *Canna. Canna. Danger comes. Men search the caves for you. Beware!*

Unsure if her own efforts would help, she remembered what Canna had taught her: *The Master is always listening. You can talk to Him any time. You should talk to Him all the time, but especially when you're in trouble. Call on Him. He loves to hear from you. He loves you.*

Canna spoke of the Master often. Gentry's father read to her from the Master's Book. The girl understood but still had her doubts. How could one Lord be everywhere all the time? Could he really hear her? Would he really answer? Why? "Because He loves you," Canna would say. But why? Gentry had a lot to figure out.

But now seemed like a good time to put Canna to the test.

Gentry bowed her head and whispered, "Please. Will you protect Canna? And me? Help her to stay away from the men who hunt her. Keep her safe. And if you will, tell her I'll meet her at Sailing Rock. She knows which one it is. The one that looks like a ship."

Gentry stopped. She bit her lip. "You know that. You know everything. Help us, please?" Something was missing from her prayer. Something Canna had insisted she always needed to add. Gentry sighed and offered a final, "Canna says I must ask for your will, not my own. But please let your will be for Canna to be safe. Amen." Something else Canna always insisted on came to mind. "And thank you." There. A complete prayer.

The girl continued to trail the two men to the caves.

The partial moonlight had passed across the river when the men reached the base of the caves, with Gentry only a short distance behind them. She would wait until they had gone into the deepest cave, then she would make a run for Sailing Rock.

The men debated which cave to search first. Francis Miller wanted to move cave by cave, exploring them all. Trelove suggested only the largest caves. Miller tried to light a torch. Trelove knocked it from his hands. "Are you a fool? The dragon will smell the smoke and see the flames. She'll be on us before you see her."

Miller snarled in a hushed voice, "What do you propose? Searching in the dark?"

"Yes. We will hear her breathing. With all the dynamite we brought, we will seal the cave until the lizard starves to death."

"Rather, we will bring the cave down on its head, crushing it for good."

Gentry's heart pounded in her chest. She had to

get to Canna. What if she were still in the caves? What if the men found Canna before Gentry did? She begged, *Please, please. Protect her. She serves you. She says you protect your children. Keep her safe. Please.* If the Lord of all the earth did indeed listen, Gentry would make sure he heard her.

The men's voices drifted off into the distance. They must have gone into the caves. Did Gentry dare sneak by? Did she dare wait instead? She had to decide.

The girl caught her lip between her teeth and stepped out. Her hands trembled. Her knees shook. She stayed in the shadows, moving along the trees until she came to the end of the forest line where there were only shrubs and scrub brush. She tucked her cloak into her pants to keep from tripping on it. She dipped down and crawled along the bank of the river, staying as hidden as she could.

Something touched her, catching her hair and pulling. Gentry stifled a scream. The girl froze. The pulling stopped. She inched forward. The pulling started again. With trembling fingers, she reached back to see what held her.

Briars on the bush had tangled in her hair. Gentry breathed out a silent sigh and pulled herself free. She made sure not to leave any trace for someone to find. No proof she'd been there. No one could know. Not even her parents. No one would be able to say Mother and Father had helped the dragon escape.

The girl crawled on the hard rock. The mud along the river would be softer but would leave a trail. No, she had to keep going. Sharp rocks pierced the skin on her knees and hands. Gentry wouldn't stop. She chewed her lip to keep from crying. Everything hurt. But she focused her thoughts on Canna. All that mattered was getting to Canna and the two of them escaping.

Voices sounded again. Gentry stiffened. She huddled under a shrub and held her breath. The men passed by her without stopping and entered the next cave. Gentry breathed without making a sound. She doubled her pace, ignoring the pain in her knees. She came to a spot where the bushes stopped. There was no cover to hide under. Gentry would have to make a run for the next shadow. And pray she didn't get caught.

The girl took several silent breaths to prepare herself. She tried to quiet the pounding of her heart. Surely the men could hear it. She could feel it in her ears. She clenched her teeth and rose to her feet. Gentry stayed doubled over, crouching low. She counted in her head, *Three…two…one.*

She sprinted off, forcing her footfalls to stay light. The rocks drew nearer…nearer…

A voice spoke in the dark. "I heard something. Something moving."

Gentry halted and hugged the ground.

Trelove's voice came back harsh. "You heard your own cowardly heartbeat. No one is here except us. And the dragon."

Francis Miller snarled, "Call me a coward? I'm out here searching for the monster."

"And running from the cave at the first excuse. What will you do when you actually face the beast? When she turns her giant head on you and pins you with her glowing eyes? Breathes fire at you? How brave will you be, Miller? You claim to have pursued her, but you've never even seen her close."

"And you have?"

"Close enough to feel her breath on my neck. I let her go once. I won't do it again. She's worth too much money."

"At least we agree on that. Dragon scales will bring a high price. And the hide is practically impenetrable. The beast will be worth millions."

"Quit running at the first sound you hear. And come with me into the next cave."

The voices faded again. Gentry rose to her feet and scampered to the shadow of the boulders. From there, she could stay in the dark and move unseen to Sailing Rock. But carefully. Oh, so carefully.

Finally, she could see the familiar shape in the distance. Carved by wind and rain, the rock looked like a sailing ship. If her prayers were answered, Canna would be near. If not, Gentry would have to return to the caves and try to beat the men to Canna.

The girl fairly flew across the final distance and hugged the massive rock in relief. She made it. But where was Canna? Gentry risked a call. "Canna? Are you here?"

She had to be. She had to be. She had…

A mound rose from the depths of the river. Canna's head broke the surface, but slowly. Her head reached up; her body followed. Up and up, she stretched. Water slipped off her in a gentle cascade, softly falling back into the river without a splash. Canna stayed in the water. No footprints.

The dragon wrapped her long neck around Gentry's body and hugged the girl. "What are you doing here, little one?"

"Men are hunting you. And Wilma Swansworth intends for me to marry her son, Brody. She is threatening my parents to get what she wants."

Tears flowed. All the fear, all the pain, all the tension from the escape poured from Gentry's eyes. She leaned her head against Canna's neck and sobbed. "I can't stay. We have to leave tonight. Now. Before the hunters find you."

"What hunters?"

"Two men. Francis Miller and a man called Trelove."

Canna's head lifted. She studied Gentry with one giant eye. "Trelove? Him?"

Gentry nodded. "He said he let you go once, but never again."

Canna snorted. "Let me go? I let him go. He came after me when I was shedding my skin. Itchy business. I trapped him and held him for three days while I wiggled out of my old crust. Then I let him go. He begged me. Told me he had a family. Children. Pleaded with me not to eat him. As if I would. I did singe his heels as he ran away. I suppose I shouldn't have, but I sneezed, and I couldn't help it."

Gentry smiled and wiped her cheeks on her sleeves. Her voice shook. "Oh, Canna. I love you."

"I love you, too, little one. Hang on to my neck. We'll leave those fools to their hunting."

Gentry wrapped her arms around Canna's thick neck. She slid down to where the dragon's neckline met her body. There, Gentry straddled Canna's body as a man rides a horse. She fixed the harness around Canna's collar and secured her pack to it. She leaned forward, wrapped the cords around her arms, and held tightly to the dragon's sinewy trunk. Canna pulled her wings from the water, shook them once, twice, and launched herself out of the river.

The dragon caught the night breeze and soared without strain into the air. Canna circled once to gain height over the rocks, then flapped and sailed over the clifftops. Another flap of her mighty wings, and they were above the treetops. Gentry's cloak flowed behind her. She could almost imagine she was flying with Canna. She could let go and…

…and fall like a stone. Gentry knew better. Imagination was wonderful, but the real world could not be ignored. But for now, just now, it was Gentry, Canna, and the wind. And it was heavenly.

* * *

CHAPTER THREE

Two days later, Gentry slid down the back of Canna's tail. The fifteen-year-old deftly avoided the spikes on the luminescent dragon's back. Canna reflected the late afternoon sunlight in rainbow colors onto the lake. Leaves in the trees whispered peace and safety. Gentry sighed and leaned against Canna's chest. "Why does everything have to be hard?"

Canna blew smoke to clear her throat. "When you're a dragon and my size, no one understands. We get blamed for everything that goes wrong. And you get blamed because you're with me."

The dragon dropped her to her side, maneuvering to prevent squashing Gentry. Canna curled her tail around the young woman. The heat from the dragon's body warmed the girl. Gentry stretched to relieve her legs after hours of holding onto Canna's sides. Flying was exhilarating, but exhausting. Gentry needed to strengthen her thighs if she were to keep up.

"Tell me again where we're going?" She picked a piece of grass and chewed on it. Not what she wanted. She wanted eggs and pancakes and sausage and all the good food her mom cooked for her. But it wouldn't happen anytime soon. Or ever again…

"Across the mountains to where dragons and people live in harmony. Where I can fly and not be shot at, and you can live and not be hated or feared because you are with a dragon."

Gentry nodded. "Right." She fell silent.

Canna curled her head around to stare Gentry in the eyes. "Are you sure you wish to come? You wish to live with me?"

"You cannot live with me, here, and I'll not leave you to live alone." Gentry stiffened her spine. "I promised you when you were a lizard no bigger than my hand. I rescued you and promised you would never be alone again."

"But you didn't know I would grow into a dragon."

"No, but what does it matter? The Book says anyone who makes a promise and stands by it, no matter what, is the one who pleases the Master."

"Except you're still a child. Your parents can change your decision."

A tear trickled down Gentry's face. "I know. But they didn't get the chance. I had to run away with you before they said anything."

Canna blew a smoke ring with another inside it. "You could go back."

Gentry shook her head. "No. I'm the girl with the dragon. Everyone hates me."

"Your parents do not hate you."

"They are the only ones. And the others will have nothing to do with me."

Canna rumbled, "Because of me."

"Because I took care of you. And I will always take care of you. You can stop arguing. I am staying with you. End of discussion. You need me, and I need you, Canna."

The dragon purred. "I love you, little one."

Gentry scowled. "I am not a child. I'm almost an adult. Marrying age, according to Wilma Swansworth." Her voice carried more sarcasm than she intended.

Canna raised the ridges above her eyes. Gentry got the message. The dragon said, "Compared to my size, you will always be a little one. But it's a term of endearment. It means I care." She held Gentry's gaze.

Gentry dropped her head. "I'm sorry. You may call me little one anytime you wish."

Canna hmphed bond added, "I should find food for you to eat. We are safe from the last town, now."

"I'm not hungry." Gentry lied, but better a little lie than Canna risking being seen in the sunlight. If it had been cloudy, she might have attempted it. But the sky was bright blue and not a cloud to be seen. Canna would be spotted quickly. No, they needed darkness or a cloudy sky for Canna to be safe. They would have to be patient.

* * *

They waited until dusk. Then they risked a low-level flight, barely clearing the treetops of the forest. Better than being seen as a glowing light in the sky and being shot at. Arrows might not pierce Canna's skin, but they might hit Gentry. Cannons would bring the dragon down, of course. If they were fired close enough to hit her. And the blunderbuss guns men used could hurt the dragon. Better to avoid being seen.

Canna landed near a deep pool in the river. Gentry disembarked and pulled Canna's harness and supply bags off for the night. Canna instructed, "Find some wood. We will need a fire for cooking."

Gentry stared at her friend. "Cooking? What are we going to cook? I thought you preferred your food raw."

Canna raised her eyelids. "Even dragons appreciate a homecooked meal now and then. And you cannot eat fish raw. Gather some dry wood and some long sticks which are still green and won't burn. I am going to catch dinner."

Gentry did as the dragon told her. She suspected she knew what Canna would do with the green sticks. But first, the dragon had to catch the fish.

Canna stared into the pool and watched. "Fish, fish, fish…here fishy, fishy."

Gentry laughed. "You call the fish? That's funny."

Canna breathed out a small puff of smoke and submerged her considerable weight into the water. She disappeared. Gentry watched. Canna wasn't a sea dragon. But she could hold her breath longer than Gentry thought possible.

A moment went by. Then two. Then three. Gentry began to worry. Was Canna safe? Had the dragon been caught on something? Should Gentry wade into the water to save her? Could she?

Suddenly Canna burst from the pool. She jumped on the shore and spit out a mouthful of large flopping fish.

Gentry's eyes widened in surprise. She counted three…five…eight. She clapped her hands. "Canna! You're amazing. But I could never eat so many."

Canna arched her neck. "They're for dinner for you tonight and tomorrow and perhaps the next day after. We'll dry them and store them in your pouch. It will give you food to eat when we can't find anything else."

Gentry hugged the dripping dragon. "You are so clever." She looked at the writhing mass on the shore. "What do we do?"

"Take a big stick and hit them in the head."

"Kill them? Canna, I've never killed anything."

Canna nodded. "I understand. But if you want to survive out here, you will have to learn. Your kind were given charge over all the creatures of the earth. Which includes fish."

Gentry stared at the slowly moving creatures. She touched one, and it jerked away from her. The girl looked at Canna, her eyes filling with tears. "I don't think I can."

Canna nodded. "I will take care of them tonight. But you'll need to be less tenderhearted if you are going to make it across the mountains. Either that or learn to eat grass."

"I tried. I can't."

"Then you will have to learn to kill to eat."

Canna smacked the fish with her tail, hard enough to kill each one without smashing it into inedible bits. The dragon instructed Gentry on how to prepare it, skewering it on the green sticks, and then holding it over the fire to cook it. Maybe because Gentry was hungry, the taste was delicious. She didn't eat all she could, though she sorely wished she had been able to. Gentry knew she'd need to save some for the next three days. Or so Canna said. And Canna was rarely wrong.

Canna slipped back to the river to catch and eat her own raw meal while Gentry cleaned the campsite. The girl took care to throw all the fish guts and scales back into the river. No one would know she'd been present. Especially with a dragon. Canna would "sweep" the ground before they took off tomorrow to make sure she left no footprints. No one would find evidence of them. As long as Canna and Gentry were careful.

The dragon came back after a short time. She showed Gentry how to lay the fish out to dry. Canna blew gently on the fillets, having Gentry flip them halfway through the drying process. It took no time to prepare the dried meals well enough so Gentry could place them in her pouch and not worry about anything spoiling.

Gentry examined the contents of her food pouch. She was down to the jerky, a handful of hard crackers, and nothing else. The girl looked at Canna. "I'll need other food soon."

Canna nodded. "Yes, you will. We'll find a town where you can barter. Get hard cheese and more crackers. Maybe some bread. And fruit, if they have any. You need fruit." Canna sighed. "I love figs. Not many shops have figs. But I would love some. Maybe the next town."

Gentry laughed. "I didn't know dragons ate figs."

Canna huffed, but only in a small way. "You would be surprised what dragons will eat."

Gentry curled beside Canna's warm belly. Canna wrapped her tail around the girl to keep her extra warm and safe. As Gentry snuggled in, she said, "Tell me. What do dragons eat?"

"All wildlife. Deer and moose and rabbits and fish. Mountain goats. Some of my kind do eat cows and sheep, but I don't. Unless I find an animal lost high alone in the wilderness. We do love sweets. Figs and apples and grapes and raisins." She stopped and added, "And chocolate. Dragons love chocolate."

Gentry sat. "Do they? Really? How do you keep it from melting when you handle it?"

"Someone must toss it to us. And since we are big and scary, there are not many people willing to feed us. Therefore, we don't get it often. But when we do…" Canna smacked her mouth and drooled a little.

It was disconcerting for Gentry, but she forced a laugh. "If I find chocolate, I'll bring it to you."

Canna rumbled in her belly. "That would be wonderful. I hear across the mountains they have chocolate that does not melt when we dragons handle it. And lots of it. All we can eat. Wouldn't that be great?"

"Won't you get too fat to fly?"

"The beautiful thing about being across the mountains. We won't worry about getting fat. We can eat and eat, and we will not gain a pound."

Gentry nodded. "I see." She didn't believe it for a minute. She'd never heard of a place where someone could eat all they wanted and not gain weight. Wonderful as it sounded, Gentry didn't believe it.

She almost didn't believe in the land across the mountains, either. Not that Canna would lie to her. But Gentry couldn't imagine a world where dragons and people could live side-by-side and not fight. It seemed too good to be true. But Canna said it, and Gentry trusted Canna. They would find out, anyhow. One day, they would find out together.

Gentry settled down under the dragon's tail. She used one part for a cushion and another part for a covering. It was warm and safe and comfortable. The girl closed her eyes. "Nite, Canna."

"Good night, little one." Canna began to hum. It wasn't a song Gentry knew, but it was peaceful and quiet and beautiful. Before long, she drifted off into sleep. And Canna sang, "Oh, how great is His love for us…" Finally, she, too, drifted off to sleep. And the moon kept watch over them both.

* * *

CHAPTER FOUR

Gentry listened to Canna's instructions for the third time. She waited until the dragon had finished, then fumed, "I understand, Canna. I understand. I know you're worried about me, but I have the directions down pat. I go into the town. I watch people walking about and talking. I listen to their conversations. When I think I've found someone who is kind, I ask them who is the most honest merchant in the area? I spend the morning comparing answers. And after I get several replies, I decide which one to go to. Unless everyone says the same thing, then I go to that person."

Gentry drew in a deep breath. "I go to the merchant. I tell him my parents are gone, and my guardian left me one precious item. But I need food, and I'm willing to trade for it. I show him the stone. I bargain for cheese and bread and crackers and fresh fruit. I give him the stone, and I get the food. I leave and come back to find you."

Canna nodded. "And if they try to make you stay?"

"I tell them I am traveling to my grandparents' home, and I'll be fine. My grandparents are expecting me. I need to keep going so they won't become worried."

Canna blew steam out of her nostrils. "I trust you to take care of yourself. But if you get into trouble…"

Gentry held up her hand. "…I ask the Master for help. He'll help me get back to you. Somehow."

Canna stretched her neck. "He has His ways. Trust Him."

Gentry folded her hands in her lap. "Does it hurt when you make the stone?"

"No." Canna dropped her head to the ground. "I have to think of something heartbreaking. I have to be very sad in order to cry. Each tear becomes a precious stone. The merchant will be happy to receive it from you and will give you what you ask for. If he's an honest merchant. But you're going to find the trustworthy one, right?"

Gentry sighed. "Yes, Canna. I'll only go to the most honorable merchant."

"He'll ask you where you got it. And you'll say…"

"I tell him my guardian gave it to me. I hate to part with it, but I need the supplies. He can keep it in exchange for the food."

Before Canna could ask another question, Gentry jumped to her feet. "It's time I left. If I'm going to find this honest merchant before nightfall, I need to be going."

"Ask for guidance. Listen closely to what the people say."

"I will, Canna."

Gentry watched the dragon shut her eyes. Canna's face became sad. Her sorrowful expression made Gentry want to cry. But the girl stood in silence. A moment later, a single tear glistened in the corner of Canna's tightly closed eye. The tear rolled from Canna's eyes to drip off her face.

Gentry caught the precious drop. It was warm to the touch, as a human tear was warm. As she stared at the tear, it cooled and became solid in her hand, forming into a single crystalline stone. It was bigger than a marble, but tear-shaped. It reflected the sun like a prism but was smooth and round. It was the most beautiful stone Gentry had ever seen. She placed the precious teardrop in her pouch for safekeeping. She asked, "What do you think about to make you so sad?"

Canna shook her head. "I won't tell you now. One day I will. But not today."

Gentry threw her arms as far as she could around the dragon's middle. "I love you, Canna. I'll see you later today. I promise."

Canna huffed a long breath. "I'll be here. Be

careful."

"I will be. I'll be back."

* * *

Gentry slipped into town behind a train of wagons all loaded with supplies and traders. Men walked beside the wagons, driving the oxen, who pulled the heavy loads. Gentry stayed behind them, anxious to see where the men would stop. Surely they would only deal with an honest merchant. Maybe she would not have to listen and ask and trust. Maybe she would simply follow the men.

Except it wasn't what Canna told her to do. Canna's way was harder and took more time.

But Canna had been very, very clear in her instructions. A small urge in her soul directed her to follow Canna's advice.

But Canna didn't know about the traders…and it was clear where they were going. The wagons stopped at the shop closest to the road. The building looked a bit rundown, the windows dirty and partially covered. A broken chair sat out in front. There was no sign telling what kind of merchant might be inside.

Gentry stood in the street for several moments, trying to decide. What should she do? What would Canna say the Master would want her to do?

The girl bent her head and muttered, "Show me what to do. Do I follow these men, or do I do what Canna said?"

A voice called out, "Child, come away from those wagons." Gentry looked. A woman stood on the plank sidewalk and waved to her. "Over here. It's not safe for you there."

One of the men driving the oxen sneered, "Don't listen to her, little girly. We won't bother you. We like children." He gave her an evil grin full of ragged teeth.

Gentry's eyes flew wide. She hustled across the road to where the woman stood. The loud jeers and crude laughs of the men made Gentry's neck crawl. She stepped on the sidewalk and approached the woman. "Thank you. I…I'm new in town. I didn't know."

"Don't worry about it now." The woman smiled. She reminded Gentry of her mother, when her mother had been younger. "What brings you into town? Where are you from?"

Gentry remembered her instructions. "I'm looking for an honest merchant. I'm going to my grandfather's village, and I need supplies. But first, I need to find a shopkeeper who will treat me fairly."

The woman's eyes glinted for a moment. Then they became kind. "My husband is the most honest merchant there is. Why don't we go together to the shop? I'll introduce you to him, and you can get your provisions there."

Gentry almost agreed but remembered Canna's directions. Canna didn't say follow the first person she found. Nor did she say trust only one voice. No, Gentry was to ask around. The girl said, "Oh, that's quite alright. I want to walk around and look in the windows before I load myself down. Thank you for helping me."

The woman pointed to a building four doors down the street. "When you're ready, my husband owns the mercantile in the whitewashed building. Mister Rendquist. He'll be happy to help you."

Gentry ducked her head and walked away. She moved along the sidewalk, following behind crowds of people, listening to their conversations. She muttered, "The woman was kind. But something in her eyes was wrong. Please, lead me to someone. To the right someone." Maybe that counted as asking the Master, even if she didn't mention his name. She meant it, anyhow.

Gentry stayed behind a group of women who went into a small storefront two doors away. A man called out from behind a counter, "Welcome, fair ladies. How can I help you this fine day?"

One woman smiled. "Greetings, Merchant William. I'm in need of fabric." She pulled out a swatch of dark-colored linen. "I need to match this as close as possible." She frowned. "Mr. Rendquist shorted me last week when I purchased material for my John's breeches." The woman shook her head. "I always buy the same amount to make a pair for him. Last week, the fabric didn't amount to enough to fit around him. I know John has gotten thinner since he had the flu, but this was ridiculous. It was barely enough fabric for a man half John's size. I asked Mr. Rendquist, but he insisted I must be mistaken. I showed him the pants, but he refused to make the matter right. Now I must match the fabric or count the whole lot lost."

Merchant William hmmed. "Let me see what I can do for you, Alice. I should have something that will match."

Gentry watched the man rummage through barrel after barrel of goods before he pulled out cloth that almost matched what Alice brought. He showed it to her. "It's the best I can do."

The woman held it, examined it, and nodded. "It is only for work breeches. It will do fine. How much?"

Merchant William shook his head. "No charge. I wouldn't bill you for something not your fault."

"Neither was it yours, William. The fault lies with Rendquist."

William laid his hand on the counter. "I've no doubt. But it doesn't mean you should pay the penalty for his..." William cleared his throat. "...error."

Alice smiled and kissed William on the cheek. "You are the kindest-hearted man I know. And the most honest. Thank you."

Gentry watched as the other women did their

business with the merchant. The shop emptied, and only the girl and the shopkeeper were left. William smiled at her. "And what can I do for you, young woman?"

Gentry held his eyes. "I'm looking for an honest merchant."

William smiled but lowered his head a touch. "I try."

"You treated those women well. I believe I can trust you." Gentry dug in her bag for the stone. She looked at William. "I need food supplies. Crackers and cheese and bread and fruit. Figs, if you have them." She stopped, then jumped in, "And chocolate." She shrugged. "If you have any."

She held out the stone. "I have this to barter. It was given me by my guardian, and it's—"

William interrupted her, his voice filled with awe. "A dragon tear."

Gentry stepped back in fear. William held up his hand. "Don't worry. Your secret is safe. May I see it?" He held out his palm.

Gentry handed it to him. He rolled the stone around, feeling it. He held the precious tear to the light. Reflections bounced off the walls. William's face broke into a smile of childlike delight. He grinned at the girl. "This is beautiful. I can't take it from you."

Gentry shook her head. "But I need the supplies. I'm going to my grandfather's, and I need food for the trip."

"I'll give you what you need for the joy of seeing one of these again. It brings back such memories."

He handed the stone back to Gentry and dug out what she requested. He put everything in her backpack. Gentry watched as the man actually teared up. She kept her voice soft. "What is it?"

William shook tears from this face. "I knew a dragon, once. He and I…bonded. But it was long ago. I'm a merchant, and he's free."

Gentry asked gently, "Where did he go?"

"The mountains. He wanted to take me with him. But I had a life here. I chose to stay behind." He looked off to the mountains. "Hardest decision of my life." He smiled, but a sad smile. "I have a wife and children now. I love them with all my heart. But the time we had, the flights we took, the adventure… I wouldn't change for anything in this world."

He patted her hand. "You put that away." He cleared his throat and lowered his voice. "Your dragon. She is nearby?"

"How do you know she's a she dragon?"

"The tears. Male dragons have amber tears. Females have white." He nodded. "You are going over the mountains?"

Gentry nodded. "That's what she tells me."

"Stay with her. Whatever you do, don't leave her. She'll take you to safety. You're an orphan?"

Gentry stared at the floor. "No. Yes. We're running away."

He placed a hand on her shoulder. "Trust her, young woman. Listen to her and trust her." He glanced outside, up both sides of the street. "You are leaving this area soon?"

Gentry nodded. "Tonight."

He sighed. "I would give anything to see a dragon again." He shook his head. "But it would be too dangerous for us to go together. People would wonder and talk."

Gentry thought hard. "Is there a place we could meet you? I don't know anything about this area. I think Canna does."

"Canna? Is she your dragon?"

"Well, more like I'm her girl. Her 'little one' she calls me."

William chuckled, but it sounded sad. "I was Tug's 'boy.' Even when I was grown, I was still his boy. It's a privilege to be called anything by a dragon. Very few people ever see them."

Gentry asked again, "Is there a place we could meet? We're by the river, where the trees are in a circle around a tall boulder."

"Round ring, we call it. If you travel up the river past the village, you will come to a broken-down bridge." William's eyes lit with longing. "I could meet you there tonight. After the first star rises past the moon. I close the shop at sunset." He lost the hope in his face. "It would be too much to ask. You best go. There are traders who would love to bring down a dragon."

The girl shook her head. "No. We'll meet you at the bridge."

He reached under the counter and dug into a small box. He lifted several smaller boxes and two cloths from its recesses. Finally, he pulled out a stone. Amber in color, Gentry could see through it. It shone like the sun. The shape was of a teardrop as Canna's had been. William handed it to Gentry. "Here. Take this to your Canna. She'll know what I say is true." He tucked it into her bag. "Now go. And don't hurry or people will wonder why you're running. Walk like you own the town. No one will bother you."

Gentry gave the merchant a quick hug, then turned and strolled out of the shop. It took everything in her not to run back to Canna with the news. But she had to be as careful returning as she had coming into town. Don't go too straight. Don't get lost. Make sure no one follows you. Be aware of all that is around you. Listen. Look.

The sun was barely still above the trees when Gentry returned to their spot at the river. Canna was nowhere to be seen. The girl slipped out of her pack and rested it against a tree. She searched the area for any sign of unwanted eyes.

Nothing. No one. She was safe.

Gentry picked up a rock and threw it into the center of the river. She stepped back and waited.

And waited. No Canna. Gentry caught another stone and threw it as well.

A small mound rose above the water. Gentry saw the top of Canna's head. An onlooker would think it was a turtle's back, nothing more. Gentry tossed another smooth stone, aiming away from Canna's head. It skipped beyond the turtle.

The dragon rose from the depths. This time, she let the water rush off her in a cascading waterfall. Canna soared up and up, mounting into the sky, then dove in a rush of air. She swooped down, backswept her wings, and touched down in a perfect landing in front of Gentry. The girl laughed. "Show off."

Canna shrugged a shoulder. "Practice." The dragon laid down on the bank to sun herself dry. "What did you find? Were you able to trade for food?"

"Better. I traded for this." She dug deep in her pack and pulled out the two tear-shaped stones. "And brought yours back." Gentry held the shining crystals. "Here." She dropped the amber rock into Canna's claws.

The dragon held the tear between her claws. She lifted it beside her eye and stared at it. And stared. And stared. Her mouth drooped. Canna looked to the sky. She rumbled a low tone. Finally, she croaked, "Tug."

Gentry stared with wide eyes. "How did you know? From a single tear?"

Canna lowered her head and placed her face even with Gentry's. "The Creator has made our tears unique, as we dragons are unique. As you are unique. I could tell from the color. It belonged to Tug." She cleared her throat. "How did you come by this?"

Gentry related her encounter with William. She finished with, "He would very much like to see you. To meet you." The girl cocked her head. "When did you meet Tug? And how did you not know William? Or know he would be in this village?"

The dragon set her head on the ground. "I met Old Tug five summers ago, when I was first stretching my wings. He taught me many tricks to flying I would not have known on my own. He was ancient and getting ready to cross the Divide. Tug didn't tell me much about his rider, only he felt abandoned. But Tug was finally ready to go across the Divide and be with others of his own kind. Where it is said we would all live as one."

Gentry eyed Canna sideways. "The divide? What is that? Is it in the mountains?"

"No. It is the Master's land. A place we go when we…pass on. It is a place of peace and safety and love and joy. Where we will all live in harmony at His feet."

Gentry hesitated, thinking hard. "Maybe it would be better if you didn't see William. If you think he abandoned Tug, it might make it hard for you."

Canna cast her eyes to the side for a moment. "No, I will see him. You told him we would come. We will. Where are we to meet him?"

"Past the village, at the broken-down bridge. He said he would be there after the first star rose above the moon."

"Let's go find this bridge. We'll hide and wait for him."

Canna stood to her feet. Gentry reached in her bag. "Wait. I almost forgot." She pulled another packet from her bag. "Figs."

Canna's eyes gleamed. She lowered her head and opened her mouth wide. Gentry grinned and tossed several of the sweet, luscious fruits into Canna's jaws.

The dragon closed her mouth, and her jaws worked the treat. She closed her eyes. The dragon moaned in delight. She launched into the air in a single bound, made a full circle in the air, and landed again. Canna smiled wide. "Ahhh…those are delicious. Wonderful. Fantastic. So good."

Gentry decided to hold back the chocolate. Canna might explode with joy. Better wait for another time. "Should we get going?"

Canna nodded, smacking her mouth. "Yes. Or else I would eat all you have and grow too big to fly. I do love a good fig."

Gentry climbed onto Canna close to her back. She leaned forward and hooked her arms in the harness. Canna turned her head around to look at the girl. "Are you ready to go?"

Gentry nodded and grasped Canna's neck. Canna looked to the sky and sprang into the air. Straight up she flew. Higher and higher she climbed until Gentry could see the layout of the land. The girl pointed to the north. "There. Is that a bridge?"

Canna leveled her flight and flapped her wings to cover the distance. The dragon's vision was ten times better than Gentry's. Canna reported, "It's a bridge. But it's not broken down."

Gentry nodded. "We'll have to keep looking."

Canna turned her head to look at Gentry. Her brilliant green eyes, with their deep flecks of black, reflected the fading sun. "We should stay low along the river. Watch for smoke. It means there are trappers or traders. Anything you see, let me know."

Gentry squeezed the dragon's neck. "I will. I'm sorry I got us into this."

Canna smiled. "I said yes. We will be fine. The Creator is watching over us."

Gentry scowled. "If he is, why did we have to run away?"

Canna continued to fly north but looked back in Gentry's eyes. "We did not *have* to run away. We *chose* to run away. You could have stayed and married Brody Swansworth."

"Ew!" Gentry shrieked. "Why would I want to do that?"

"I didn't say you would want to. But you could have. The Master doesn't *make* us do things. He allows us to make our own choices. Rather than marry Brody, you chose to leave. Rather than face Francis Miller and Trelove, I chose to leave with you. I could have stayed."

"But they wanted to kill you."

"I still could have stayed. I could have fought them. I could have maybe killed them. I could have set fire to the whole town. I could have done a thousand things. But I chose to go with you. The Maker of all things let me make the choice. And now, He watches over us in our choices."

Gentry thought it over. "It would have been easier if he had simply made Francis Miller not hate you."

Canna turned her head north and flew for a few wing strokes. She turned around again. "Do you like Francis Miller?"

"No." Gentry made it emphatic. "He's detestable."

"Do you want the Master to *make* you like him?"

Gentry shook her head. "No! Of course not. Why would he do that?"

"Why is a question only He gets to ask and answer. Do you want Him to make you marry

Brody?"

"No!"

"You want to be free to choose."

Gentry considered where Canna was going with the conversation. "If I want to be free to choose, I have to let other people make their choices."

"Even when they are bad ones. It's what He has decreed. We get to choose. We can choose to do His will, or we can choose to follow our own path. He will ultimately have His plan done, but in the meantime, we get to make choices."

Gentry looked at the dragon's middle. "Even bad ones."

"Even those." Canna turned around and looked ahead. "I see another bridge. Or the ruins of one. It must be the one William spoke of."

Canna banked her flight and glided in for a landing. Gentry dismounted and ran to the ruins. "This looks right. Unless there's another one. But William would have known and said something. This must be it."

Canna ordered, "Gather some dry wood. You'll need a fire for him to find you."

The girl scouted around. She pulled old wood from the bridge pilings to use for her fire. She dragged it onto the shore where Canna would light the blaze. The dragon blew on the logs, and in moments, a blazing fire erupted. The wood was dry. There would be little smoke. Only a column of heat and light.

Gentry heard the rattle of wooden wheels on the dry dirt road. She hissed, "Hide, Canna." The dragon dived into the river and disappeared. Gentry sat, settled her pack beside her, and waited. She buried her nervousness with several long, slow breaths. Relax. It was probably William. Nothing to be anxious about. Right.

The wagon appeared around the bend. The rattles came more from the cargo than the wheels. Overloaded with trinkets hanging from the sides and piled high with items to trade, it clattered and banged as it rolled along. The wagon was pulled by two skinny oxen. They moved along at a set pace, lowing as they went. The wagon came from the north, headed south.

Beside the wagon walked a withered man with a battered hat that covered most of his face. He bellowed at the beasts of burden, "Get up there, lazy cows! Ol' Bailey needs to get to Trimor by nightfall. Can't be out with all the cutthroats and villains who inhabit this forest at night. Get up there." He cracked a whip over the animals' heads. Neither ox paid him any attention. They continued their slow, steady pace.

The man looked out from under his hat and caught Gentry's eyes. He shouted, "Whoa, boys. Whoa. What does Ol' Bailey see? Who is this?"

Gentry stood. "Good evening, sir."

The man muttered, "She calls Ol' Bailey 'sir.' She doesn't know, does she? Hmm. What is she doing here, hmm? Alone like this? No one around but her?"

Gentry kept her voice from shaking. "I'm not alone. I have a friend with me."

"Ol' Bailey doesn't see any friends. Just a girl." The man moved closer to stare at Gentry.

Gentry put more force in her voice. "He's out hunting dinner. He'll be back soon."

The man stepped back a moment, then squinted his eyes. "Maybe we'll wait for this friend. See what he brings back for dinner. Maybe Ol' Bailey can share. Maybe." The old man crouched beside his wagon and leaned against the side for support. He took out a long pipe from his pocket and began to chew on it. No smoke came, just the sound of air being sucked in and out.

Gentry moved to put the fire between herself and Bailey. Safer. What should she do? Would Canna have to make an appearance to scare the man off? Could Gentry talk the man into leaving?

After a few uncomfortable moments, Gentry suggested, "Shouldn't you be going if you want to be in Trimor before dark?"

"What does she know of Ṭrimor, hmm? Little girl like her, out here on her own."

Gentry's voice snapped. "I'm not a little girl. And I'm not here alone. I told you. I have a friend nearby."

Bailey rubbed his pipe in his hands. "So, she says. I see no friend. I see one pack. Where's her friend's pack, hmm? Don't see boot marks. Just her."

The girl evened out her tone. "He walks softly. Leaves no tracks. It's how we were taught." She continued, "I was in Trimor today. If that's the name of the next village on your route, I saw traders there already. You might want to get there soon, in order to sell what you have before they do."

Bailey laugh was harsh. "Always a market for what Ol' Bailey sells, isn't there, now?"

The man lunged forward, straight through the fire, and grabbed Gentry before she could react. He hauled her to her feet, his hands like vices on her arms. "Pretty little girl like her? Ol' Bailey will get a good price for her. Always a buyer for a servant. Or a slave." He cackled as he dragged her toward the wagon.

Gentry struggled against him. She flailed and kicked and wrestled and screamed and did all she could to get free. Nothing worked. She was trapped.

* * *

CHAPTER FIVE

"Let her go!" a deep male voice yelled across the clearing. Old Bailey stopped moving toward the wagon but didn't let go of Gentry. William shouted again, "Let the girl go!"

The tattered man laughed. "No worries here. No worries. Just Ol' Bailey and his little girl. Having an argument, see. Her's trying to run away. Ol' Bailey's taking her home."

William reached the man. "She's not your daughter. I know her. Take your hands off her, now."

Bailey dropped his arms from around Gentry. He shoved her to the ground and grabbed a knife from his pocket. He lunged at William, who sidestepped the jab. The merchant knocked the knife down, but the trader grabbed it before William could kick it away. Gentry scrambled to her feet and ran to the wagon. She unhooked the oxen and yelled, "Hie! Get up!"

Whether because there was something different

in her voice or because they felt the weight lifted, the two oxen took off lumbering down the road. They stopped a short distance away.

Bailey turned and hollered, "Hold up there! What's she doing?"

William took the moment to kick the old man's legs out from under him and dived on his knife hand. Bailey twisted and stabbed William in the arm. Gentry screamed and rushed to help her defender.

At that moment, the river erupted. A sudden tornado of water surged from the banks high into the air. Everyone turned to see what was happening.

Canna roared from the depths, climbing straight up, high into the sky. She turned and dived back down, snatching Bailey in her mouth. She beat her massive wings, gained height, and disappeared over the trees. Bailey's screams faded off into the distance.

Gentry turned to William in horror. "She's not going to eat him, is she?"

William shook his head. "I doubt it. She's going to scare him, though. And drop him far enough from people, he can't tell anyone for some time. If anyone would believe him."

Gentry dug through Bailey's wagon and found cloth to use to bandage William's arm. She wrapped it carefully around the wound. They made themselves comfortable by the fire to wait for Canna's return. The flames crackled and popped.

Smells of pine perfumed the air.

An hour passed, and Canna flew back to join them, landing near the river. The dragon glided in, making sure to leave no tracks or ruts with her clawed feet. There was no sign of Bailey.

Gentry rushed to Canna and hugged her middle. "Oh, Canna. I was so scared. You were magnificent!"

Canna snorted. Little wisps of smoke puffed from her nostrils. "Humph. I should have fried him. Trying to steal a person and sell her into slavery. I should have—"

William interrupted her. "You should have done what you did. Carried him off to parts unknown."

Canna eyed William closely. "You are the merchant from town? William? You protected my little one. Thank you. Are you wounded severely?"

William shook his head. "My arm. It will heal. I may have a time explaining to my wife what happened, but the arm will be fine."

Canna settled onto her haunches. "Let me see the wound."

William held up his arm. "Gentry did a fine job of bandaging it. I'm sure—"

Canna spaced her words. "Let. Me. See. The. Wound."

William bowed his head. "Yes, ma'am." He unwrapped the bandage Gentry had carefully applied.

Canna narrowed her eyes at the jagged tear. She looked at William, then at the wound. The dragon closed her eyes for a moment. She sat silent, her mighty neck bowed. She lifted her head and opened her eyes. She breathed in through her nose, held it, and breathed out a vapor directly on the cut. A small cloud formed around the injury. It covered the cut. Canna exhaled out and out…then leaned back.

The cloud cleared. William and Gentry stared at the wound…or where the wound had been. There was nothing there. The gash was healed. Not even a scar remained.

William's eyes flew wide. As did Gentry's. They looked at the arm, looked at each other, and looked at Canna. William stuttered, "How?"

Canna shrugged. "I have been given the gift of healing. I only use it when allowed. I must ask first. Which I did. I was told yes. This time."

William flexed his arm, moved it all around, and smiled wide. "It's perfect. It's better than before."

Canna nodded. "The Creator does all things well, Merchant William."

William laughed. "Yes, yes, He does." He made a sweeping bow before Canna. "It is my deepest pleasure to meet you, Mistress Canna. I have wanted to see another dragon for years. I feared you had all gone to the Divide and were all gone from this earth."

Canna shook her head. "Not all. Many. Maybe most. But not all of us." She swung her head to indicate Gentry. "She and I will be going over the mountains. It is getting harder to live here. The others of my kind are high in the mountains, or across the oceans. They have yet to be hunted as I am."

William nodded. "I understand. Two men came through the village some days ago. They were looking for you. Not you, but asking if anyone had seen a dragon."

Gentry eyed Canna. The girl's gaze widened, then narrowed. Canna raised the ridges above her eyes. "Two men, you say. Did they happen to identify themselves?"

"One said his name was Francis—"

"—Miller." Canna's voice hardened. "And did the other name himself as Trelove?"

William rubbed his palm on his leg. "You know these men?"

Gentry couldn't contain her anger. "They want to kill Canna. They want to cut her up and sell her parts. Trelove says he wants to pull all her teeth and trade them for some reward."

William wiped his hand across his face. "You shouldn't stay in this area. You should be going. Now. Tonight. I'm sorry I delayed you. But I longed to see a dragon again. To remind myself Tug and I really did have time together. He did exist."

Canna lowered her head so she could look William in the eye. "Take back your tear. Only great love can cause enough pain to make a dragon cry.

Tug must have loved you very much to give you his tear."

Gentry dug out the tear from her backpack. She handed it to William. The man held up his hand to stop her. "I don't deserve it. I abandoned him. I sent him to the mountains alone."

Canna's face took on a sly grin. "Humans don't abandon dragons. We allow them to leave if they choose. But we are never abandoned. Tug is no longer alone. Be assured, across the Divide, there are no tears, no regrets, no longing for things past. There is only joy. Be at peace, Merchant."

William bowed his head. "I thank you for the gift of your wisdom, Canna. I will hold what you say in my heart against the times I long to see Tug again."

Canna continued, "The Master has promised all who He calls will be with Him across the Divide. And will live forever with Him. You'll see Tug again."

Gentry yawned and instantly covered her mouth. "I'm sorry. I'm tired."

William nodded. "You've had a hard day. I will leave you two now so I can get home before my wife misses me."

Canna laid her taloned foot on top of William's head with extreme care. She intoned, "Go with the blessing of the Creator, Merchant William. He holds you in His hands." She released him. Gentry hugged the man, and he slipped away into the forest and the night.

Gentry watched him go and turned to Canna. The girl spied the trader's wagon. "What about his stuff, Canna? What should we do with it?"

Canna moved the wagon into the center of the clearing. "I will leave this for others to find. Let them do as they wish. I will not touch it."

"What about the oxen?"

Canna frowned. "We will let them go. They will either find their way back to town or will be found by someone."

"You're not going to eat them?" Gentry's heart melted at the thought.

"I could. They're half-starved, and if there's any chance Bailey found them to take them back, I would spare them. See if they are marked."

"Why?"

"It may be they were stolen to begin with. If you find a mark with a bar through it, oftimes it is a sign the beast belongs to someone. The second mark is an attempt to hide the original owner's brand."

Gentry approached the two oxen. The tan beasts stood still and silent, apparently used to being handled. Gentry took the torch and checked over their flanks. Nothing. The girl looked up at Canna. "No marks."

"Look under their thighs. Sometimes an owner will try to hide the brand. It makes them easier to get back if they're stolen. And the thieves don't look there."

Gentry wondered again how Canna knew all she did. Often her answer was a simple, "The Master." How the Master taught the dragon was still a mystery Gentry had yet to solve. The girl bent down and looked carefully under the first ox. No mark. The second ox had two Os with an X over them, It made the Os hard to see.

She stood up and reported her findings. Canna shook her head. "If one was stolen, it is likely both were, even if the second isn't marked."

Gentry bit her lip. "What are we going to do?"

"Set them free and let someone find them. They can look for the owners. We will be free from any guilt." Canna sighed. "I was looking forward to roast beef. But fish will suffice."

Gentry stroked Canna's head. "I'm sorry, Canna."

"No, you're not. You would keep the oxen as pets. I know your heart."

"I kept you."

"I am hardly a pet." Canna sniffed.

Gentry laughed. "No, you're not." She grew sober. "What will leave the oxen here?"

"I'll fly them away to where they can graze and eat and be safe until someone finds them."

Gentry eyed Canna. "You won't eat them, right?"

Canna held Gentry's gaze. "A child of the

Master does not lie, Gentry. I promised I would not lie to you. You must never lie to me, either. If you can't trust me in the little things, how will you trust me in anything important?"

Gentry lowered her head. "I'm sorry, Canna. You're right. You've never lied to me. I promise I won't ever lie to you, either."

Canna nodded her head once. She waddled over to the oxen and picked up the first one. It bellowed and lowed and kicked, but Canna held it firmly in her claws, being careful not to pierce its hide. She leaped into the air and took flight.

Gentry sat down beside the fire. It might be a long night. She should get comfortable. The near capture by Bailey, the rescue by William, the healing of his arm…it had been a full few hours. She settled against her pack and watched the fire. She closed her eyes for a moment.

* * *

She must have fallen asleep, because she heard Canna calling, "Little one. Gentry. Wake, child."

Gentry found herself on the ground. The fire had burned low and was almost out. She stretched, all her limbs aching. "Is it done?"

"It is done. We must be going." Canna swirled the fire around with her foot to put the embers out. Gentry fetched water from the river and poured it on the ashes. Canna blew her hot breath on the mud to dry it. No one would know someone had been camping there. Everything looked as it had before Canna and Gentry arrived. Only the abandoned wagon remained.

Gentry picked up her pack, climbed on Canna's back, worked her way to her riding position, and hung on. Canna leaped into the air, blew away any remaining footprints, turned, and headed high into the sky. The stars shone bright and cold. Gentry asked, "Which way do we go?"

"First star on the right, then straight on 'til morning."

"What?"

Canna shook her great head. "Never mind. We will fly until daybreak. We will find a place to settle in for a few days. I can't fly day after day without a rest."

"I understand." Gentry laid her head against the dragon's neck. "I love you, Canna." Gentry curled under her cloak and let the flapping of Canna's wings rock her. She heard the dragon singing softly, "Sing Hallelujah to the Lord. Sing Hallelujah to the Lord. Sing Hallelujah…" The dragon flew on.

* * *

CHAPTER SIX

"Canna, do we have to fly in the rain?" Gentry tried not to complain. But her cloak was soaked, her tunic was soaked, her skin was soaked… They'd been flying through the downpour for half the night. The girl was cold, she was wet, and she was miserable.

"We'll stop at dawn and make camp. We can light a fire and get everything dry."

"How? It won't stop raining." Gentry didn't bother to keep the whine out of her voice. The rain had caught the two by surprise. In the dark, the dragon couldn't find a suitable cave. Nor could they risk landing in the unknown territory. Too much chance of being spotted and hunted. "I can light a fire that will burn underwater if I must."

Gentry didn't believe the dragon could, but also didn't want to call Canna a liar. Not to her face. Or back. Gentry sighed, adjusted the straps on the harness around her, and held on tighter. At least the wind had stopped battering the dragon, making progress difficult. They'd fought a headwind for two days, and the gale had only let up in the evening.

Dragon and girl only traveled after dark. Safer for Canna that way. She landed as the last star disappeared in the sky, before dawn had begun to lighten the horizon. They traveled along another riverbank until Canna found a suitable place to bed down for the day. The dragon always looked for caves or overhangs in the cliffs to act as shelter from beating sun, pelting rains, or searching eyes.

As dawn approached, they found a cave halfway up a cliff. With a little effort, Canna was able to reach the opening and use her powerful sense of smell to determine the cave was unoccupied. She wedged her body into the small space for the day. There was room enough for Gentry to stand, but Canna had to crouch.

Gentry climbed off Canna's back, wrung out her cloak and tunic. Canna instructed her, "Spread all your clothes on the rocks by the opening. I'll dry them tonight, and they'll be warm when you put them on."

Gentry obeyed. It felt good to climb out of the soggy apparel. Canna curled and laid in a warm circle. She asked, "How are we doing for food supplies?"

Gentry frowned. "We're about out again."

Canna scowled. "I'll go fishing this afternoon

and dry the fish tonight."

Gentry sighed. "Can we find something other than fish?" She stopped quickly. "I'm not complaining, Canna. I know you supply all my needs. But it would be wonderful to have food besides fish for a change."

"I could hunt deer. Do you know how to fix it?"

Gentry lowered her head. "No. I watched Mother cook it one time, but after seeing Father butcher the animal, I had no appetite for it. I was young. I think I could learn now."

"This from the girl who didn't want me to kill the oxen." Canna smirked.

Gentry frowned. "I will accept whatever you provide for me and be grateful." The girl stopped. "But is it wrong to want something else, something more?"

"Something else, no. Something more, yes."

Gentry cocked her head. "I don't understand. What's the difference?"

"If the Master has yet to supply anything and you ask for something other than fish, that is fine. If He has provided fish and you want more than fish, that is not okay. In that instance, you're saying what He has given you isn't good enough. You want something more. Do you understand?" Canna blew out her nose and tendrils of smoke curled in the air.

Gentry mulled it over in her mind. "I think I see. If I ask before he provides, it's okay. If I ask after he gives me food, I'm complaining and not being grateful. I understand the difference." She hesitated. "Since we need food, it's okay to ask for something besides fish, right?" The girl stretched to try to get more comfortable. One of Canna's scales was sticking in Gentry's elbow.

"Yes, little one. Food has not been provided at this time. You can ask Him about other meat." Canna ruffled and her scales lay down flat.

Gentry stared at Canna for a long moment. "He knows everything. Doesn't he already know what I want?" She cocked her head to watch Canna's eyes.

"Yes, but He wants you to ask. He longs to talk with you. Asking for even the little things, like food, gets you in the habit of talking to Him. It's not hard to ask Him for big things." The dragon nodded a tad.

"Are there things that are big to him?" Gentry couldn't imagine what they could be.

"No. But He knows there are to you. He wants you to ask about those too. Things like help when you're in trouble. Asking to let me hear you from a distance. Saving you from Old Bailey. You consider those big things. They are no bigger than asking for meat other than fish to Him. He is Lord of the Universe, Gentry. We are as a grain of sand on the beach. But He cares about every hair on your head. You are that precious to Him."

Canna began to hum in her wordless way. It reminded Gentry of her mother and home. She wondered what her parents were thinking. Were they worried about her? Missing her? Was she right to leave without saying a word? Gentry sighed. She leaned into the dragon for warmth and comfort and fell asleep.

She was woken by Canna's voice calling, "Gentry, Gentry. Time to wake, little one."

Gentry stretched her arms and legs, curling her toes under for good measure. She rolled onto her feet and stood. The girl looked out of the cave. "Canna, it's still light out."

"I know. But I need to talk to you."

The dragon's voice had an air of seriousness to it Gentry had seldom heard. She studied Canna's face. "What's wrong?"

Canna shifted slightly. "I had a message from Curves. He says there's trouble, and he needs help."

"Curves? Who is Curves? And what kind of message?" More important, what kind of trouble? Something that would cause Canna to fly in daylight had to be serious.

"Curves is a fellow dragon. A friend of mine. I met him a few years ago. When I was still learning about being a dragon. He taught me to fly. Not to fly, but to *fly*. He's a tremendous flier." She stopped. "We have talked mind-to-mind, like when you told me about the hunters. He says there is trouble where the dragons live. He needs me to come."

"We should go."

Canna hesitated. "That's the problem. It's the opposite direction from the mountains where we were going. It's closer to the home where your parents are living."

Gentry tried to sort out what Canna wasn't saying as much as what she was. The girl asked, "Why is that a problem? I go where you go."

Canna shook her giant pearl head. "It is one thing for us to encounter trouble and danger as we are going to the mountains. It is another thing for me to take you knowingly where there may be danger."

"But if I say I want to go, that's what matters."

"Is it? What about what the Master thinks? What He wants? Don't those things matter to you?"

Gentry sat back with her legs crossed. "I didn't think about that." She fell silent. "We should ask him, shouldn't we?"

"That would be a good thing."

Gentry bowed her head and closed her eyes. The girl waited for Canna to ask, but the dragon remained silent. After several moments, Gentry asked, "Aren't you going to ask him?"

"I already did. He is waiting for you to speak with Him."

"Oh." Gentry shifted in her seat, suddenly uncomfortable. She hesitated, then asked, "How will I know what he answers?"

"Ask Him first. Wait for the answer. A good father will make sure his children understand his answer."

The girl lowered her head again. She studied the ground, looked at Canna's feet, looked out of the cave, then asked, "What if I don't like his answer?"

"You should talk to Him before you worry about what you will like and what you won't."

"But what if he tells me no?"

"What if He does? Will you still obey Him? I will."

Gentry hadn't thought about Canna obeying. Only about her own battle. She sighed, and admitted, "If you're going to obey him, and I have to go with you, what good is it for me to ask?"

"He wants to hear from you, little one. Even if He tells you no, He still wants to hear from you. A 'no' answer is still one given in love."

"What did he tell you?"

"Talk to Him, Gentry." The sternness in the dragon's tone left no room for argument.

Gentry lowered her head again. "Master, I'm sorry I don't talk to you like you want me to. I'd like to go with Canna to help her friend Curves. Would you please allow me to go?"

The girl sat silent for several moments. A strong impression came over her she needed to go home and tell her parents where she was. She'd been wrong to run off and not say anything. She should go home. And once she'd done that, maybe, just maybe, she would be able to go with Canna. But first she had to go home.

But what if she went home and her parents said no?

What if they say yes?

What if—

You'll never know if you don't go home and find out.

Gentry opened her eyes. She looked at Canna. "You know what he said, don't you? I have to go home and talk to my parents."

"I knew. He told me I was wrong to take you away without telling your parents. I should have made you go back that night." The dragon swung her head side to side. "I was worried about the men, but it was not an excuse. So, we will go back and tell your parents why we ran away. They can decide what we should do."

Gentry sighed. "But it will take a long time to get there. We've been flying for days."

Canna shrugged her shoulder. "When He told me I was wrong, I started flying in circles near your home. Flying at night kept you from noticing. We will be home before breakfast."

"Canna!" Gentry exploded. "Why didn't you tell me?"

"You weren't ready to hear it. You must admit you've missed your parents. You wouldn't have been as willing to return if you didn't."

Gentry nodded. "I do miss them. And I should

have trusted them." She stood, picked up her tunic and leggings, and put them on. "They aren't going to make me marry Brody Swansworth, are they?"

"What do you think?"

The girl admitted, "I don't think my father would ever agree to it. I was afraid of what Wilma Swansworth would do to them."

Canna blew warm air to make sure Gentry's clothes were dragon-approved for flying. "I think your parents would do anything to keep you from being unhappy. No matter what Wilma Swansworth threatened to do. If it were your daughter, would you?"

"I'd sell out and move rather than make my daughter marry someone she doesn't like."

"You have your answer."

They waited until sundown before leaving the cave. Gentry climbed the scales on Canna's leg to reach her riding spot, put the harness around Canna's neck, and strapped in. Canna crawled out of the cave, let herself fall down the cliff, opened her wings, and took flight.

Canna was right. In the dark, Gentry had no idea where they were or which way they were headed. If she had watched the direction of the stars, she might have had some clue they were still close to home or flying in circles. But she'd been too busy admiring the beauty.

The night sky burst with more stars than there

were grains of sand along the river. Brilliant blazing ones. Small ones twinkled and seemed to blink in and out. Others stayed unmoving. Some looked very close indeed. Some were so far away they appeared like a pin prick in the black of night. All of them too wonderful to worry about which position they were in.

Looking down, the land was dark and empty. Every now and again there was a lone cottage or farm, illuminated by a fire in a fireplace, or a lantern on a table. Not that Gentry could see inside the houses, but she came to recognize the glows for what they were.

Canna flew for half the night. Gentry studied the land and decided the dark ribbon dividing the cabins and villages must be the river. They followed its contours for what seemed like hours. Gentry didn't sleep. Worry about seeing her parents again, worry about meeting with Francis Miller and Trelove, worry about what Wilma Swansworth would say or do, all kept her awake. The girl would settle one worry only to have a different one arise. Like playing "Bop the puppet" at the fair…hit one, it goes down, but another one comes up. Hit it, and a different puppet comes to the surface. She couldn't keep them all down.

Finally, she leaned forward for Canna to hear her. "Canna, how do I stop all these fears? I'm scared about going back. Scared what Mother and Father will say. Scared what Wilma Swansworth will say. Scared Francis Miller or Trelove will find you. How do I stop being scared?"

Canna turned her head to look at Gentry, flying forward but gazing backward. "You can't on your own. You must trust the Master. He promises to work everything for your good. It may be hard, and it may not look good at the start, but in the end, all things will work for good. It takes faith, little one. Trusting He is good, and He loves you. He only wants what's best for you. Believe Him."

"Do all dragons trust him?"

"Not all of us. Like people, we must make the decision to follow Him."

"When did you meet him?"

Canna smiled, and her eyes took on a faraway look. She turned her head to the front, adjusted her angle of flight, then turned back to explain, "It was one of my trips away, when I was learning to fly. Curves and I had been out flying, and I got lost. I didn't know where I was or how to get back. I didn't know how I was ever going to find my way home. And night came, and it grew terribly dark. I couldn't see anything. Dragons see without light, but there was nothing to see. Only blackness. I was alone. I was scared. And I cried out for help.

"That's when He surrounded me with His light. He told me He loved me and wanted me to be with Him. I could say no, but that would mean I'd still be lost and alone. I told Him I wanted to be with Him forever. He brought me home, taught me about His ways, and I've been following Him ever since. And He's never left me."

Gentry mulled over Canna's words. "Do you have to be alone and in a dark place to follow him? Do I have to get lost first?"

"No, little one." Canna smiled. "Not at all. You only need to admit you want to follow Him and ask Him to be your Master. He will meet with you and teach you what He wants you to do. He wants you to be full of light and life and joy and peace."

Gentry sighed. "That would be wonderful." She hesitated. "Does following him mean I can't do everything I want to do?"

"Following Him means you start wanting to do what He wants you to do. Not because you have to, but because you get to. You want to do what makes Him happy. Because in the end, it makes you happy, too."

"You like serving him?"

"I love serving Him."

Gentry pursed her lips. She leaned back in her straps and grew silent. Canna turned her head around and flew straight again. Gentry went back to watching the river.

They flew for what seemed like another hour before Canna dropped lower and closer to the treetops. Gentry could see the faintest outlines of the sunrise beginning to lighten the sky. Canna glided like a giant swan into a landing on the river. She paddled with her feet until she reached land.

Gentry recognized the caves near home. The dark mound must be Sailing Rock. Canna's cave loomed ahead. The dragon lumbered into the opening and sniffed. She narrowed her eyes. "Men have been here, but not for many days. We're safe for today. You can walk home from here, and I will wait for you."

Gentry slid down off the dragon's back. Her fear came back full force. "What am I going to say to Mother and Father? How do I explain why I ran away? What if—"

Canna interrupted her. "You won't know what they will say until you go home. You won't have to guess. Ask the Master to help you. He will give you words to say. But I suggest you start with, 'I'm sorry.' And maybe, 'I love you.' Those two sentences always seem to help."

Gentry smiled in spite of her fear. "You're right. I'll go."

"Be careful. And come back when you can. I'll be here."

"You be careful. Those men may still be around." Gentry gave Canna a warm hug. "I'll be back soon. I promise."

Gentry left her pack of food and her special things with the dragon. She would come back for them. And maybe need them on the next flight.

The girl slipped through the tree line. The half-light of dawn let her tell the stumps from the holes and the rocks from the bushes. She listened at every clearing before crossing. The only sounds were the birds and squirrels. Nothing else moved.

She came out around the shrubs to see the house still standing. Why she'd imagined it wouldn't be was one of those fears she needed to give up. Of course it would still be standing. Where was it going to go?

Gentry didn't try to answer the question. Her heart tugged at her. She didn't realize how much she missed her mother and father. The girl ran toward the back of the house, only to stop at the sound of a voice. Father.

"I've told you before, Wilma, I don't know where Gentry is. I'm sure it had to do with you insisting she marry your son. As fine a young man as you say he is, he'll have no trouble finding a wife over in Belling. That's why you sent him there, isn't it? To find a wife?"

Gentry hid behind the garden fence. She heard Wilma Swansworth's voice but couldn't make out the words. Father spoke again.

"Your son is your problem. Perhaps he's not ready to settle down. I told you the children were too young to think of marrying. And my daughter made it clear she had no interest in your son. I would no more force her to marry him than I would force her to marry my prize sheep. And I love my sheep."

Gentry clapped her hand over her mouth to keep from laughing. Love for her father poured through her. She'd been wrong to run away without telling them.

Wilma droned something. Father said, "You do what you must do, Wilma. But remember, we from the southside were here before you came, and will be here after you're gone. You may own the town, but you do not own my family. If Gentry had to choose between marrying Brody and running, I'd tell her to run as far and as fast as she could. Now, you can see yourself off my property."

Wilma apparently had something more to say. Father snorted. "Your dragon hunters have about as much chance of finding Canna as you did of finding Gentry. I don't doubt the dragon and my daughter are together. I'd have them both here if it were up to me. But since you've seen fit to make it impossible, I will be satisfied with knowing they're both safe and away from you. Good morning, Ms. Swansworth."

Wilma passed the garden wearing an expression that would curdle fresh goat's milk. Gentry stayed low and hidden until she saw the widow cross the bridge to her own side of the river. Gentry stole her way into the house to grab her father and catch him in a bear hug. Gentry buried her face in her father's shoulder and cried. "Father. Oh, Father."

Father began crying. He kept his voice low but called out, "Mother! Our daughter is back. Gentry is home."

Mother came running from the back of the house. She threw her arms around both Father and Gentry, swallowing them in an excited embrace.

How long they stood and held each other and cried, Gentry didn't know. All that mattered was they were together again. When at last Father stopped crying, Mother dried her tears. She wiped the moisture from Gentry's face. "Where have you been, child?"

Father led Gentry and Mother to the bench in the kitchen where they could all sit. Gentry sat between her mother and father as they continued to hold her. The girl wiped her face with the back of her sleeve. "Away. With Canna. She took me flying." Gentry stared at the ground. "Canna made me see I was wrong for running away." Gentry bit her lip, then admitted, "I was afraid you would make me marry Brody Swansworth. Wilma would get her way, and I'd have to be Brody's wife to save the farm. I didn't want to marry him, and I thought if I ran away, Wilma couldn't do anything to you. But Canna made me come back. I'm sorry I ran away."

Father kissed the side of Gentry's head. "I would never see you wed to someone you didn't love, no matter what Wilma Swansworth threatened. I'd rather lose everything than see you unhappy."

Gentry held her father's eyes. "And I didn't want you to lose everything. I thought the best answer was to run off. No one could accuse you of hiding me or knowing where I was." She looked at her mother. "I'm sorry."

Mother kissed her. "I understand. I'm happy Canna brought you back."

Father held Gentry's hand. "I need to know. Did the dragon suggest you run away?"

Gentry shook her head hard. "No. No. It was my idea. I wasn't thinking about leaving in the beginning. I thought about living at the caves, maybe coming back every now and then to see you. But when I went to the caves where Canna was, I came across two men who were hunting Canna. Francis Miller and a man named Trelove. They wanted to kill her and cut her up and sell her parts for a reward."

Gentry's voice became fierce. "That's when I knew we had to leave. I didn't want to marry Brody or have anything happen to Canna. We flew to Trimor. That's as far as we got, I think. Canna began flying in circles until I realized I needed to come home and face you both."

Gentry glanced from her mother to her father. "It wasn't Canna's fault. Honest. She protected me. She made sure I was safe and had food and shelter. We even made a friend along the way." The girl pleaded, "Don't be mad at her, please."

Father frowned. He opened his mouth, then

stopped. He looked at Mother and began to chuckle. A moment later he was bent over laughing until tears ran down his cheeks. Mother and Gentry exchanged confused and almost frightened looks. What was he thinking?

Father stopped, sat straight, and wiped his face. He did not stop chuckling, however. "Oh, my child. I was about to say I expected more maturity from a dragon, and it hit me. I was expecting maturity from a *dragon*! A beast! I was going to blame the creature for you running away. As if a horse could convince you to leave us. No, Gentry, it is not the dragon's fault. I don't blame her."

Gentry continued to stare at her father with concern. She didn't know quite what to say. Should she defend Canna from the "beast" designation? Or let it go and leave well enough alone? The girl nodded slowly. "I'm happy to hear that."

"No, the fault lies with your mother and me for not defending you from Wilma Swansworth more vehemently that night. If we had, you wouldn't have thought your only choice was to run away. For that, I apologize. You don't ever have to worry about that again. You will never, ever, marry Brody. No matter what Wilma may do to us. Let her try her worst."

Gentry hugged her father, then her mother. Mother nodded with Father. "I'm sorry as well, Gentry. We should have thrown the woman out of the house. She will never step foot in here again, you can believe me."

Gentry sighed with happiness. "Thank you. Thank you. I knew you loved me. I didn't want anything to happen to you. I thought she would try to buy you out, or run you out, or do something to make you have to leave."

"She can try. Let her. I welcome it." Father's face hardened.

"But the dragon hunters?"

Father shook his head. He kissed the side of Gentry's face. "Your dragon should be safe. I doubt either man could find his way out of a tunnel with but one exit. They've been chasing rumors all over the district looking for you."

Father lowered his head. "I'll confess, I was anxious to hear their reports. To know if they had found any trace of you. But they never did. The closest they came was a tale from Pence. Someone had seen a shadow by the river that might have looked like the form of a dragon. But it was night, and there was no moon. They couldn't be sure."

Gentry's heart relaxed. Pence? She'd never heard of it. And the night with no moon had been but a week ago. They'd still been near Trimor. But she would tell Canna about it anyhow. Even a rumor could be trouble for the girl's best friend.

"You forgive me for running off with Canna? You don't hold it against her, either?"

"No, child." Father spoke first. Mother shook

her head in agreement. "Not against either of you. But do not do it again without talking to us. We could have straightened this out before you felt you had to leave."

"I love you both." Gentry hugged her parents. Now, how could she tell them she wanted to fly off with Canna again?

CHAPTER SEVEN

Three days later, Gentry took Father to meet with Canna. They climbed down the cliffs to the caves. The river ran merrily as it always did. There were no signs of any dragon hunters.

Canna lay sunning herself on the riverbank. She rose as Father and Gentry arrived. The dragon bowed low to him. "I am honored, sir. I am more honored that you trust your daughter to my care."

Father scoffed but smiled. "I am not sure I have a choice. She has her own mind, it seems." His eyes twinkled, however. A fish jumped in the swift water.

Canna nodded. "She does. But you are still her parent, and she lives under your roof. While there, she obeys you. It is what the Master has decreed."

Father raised his eyebrows. "When Gentry said you served the Creator, I thought she meant as any beast does." He eyed her sideways. "But you know Him? Know His laws?"

Gentry cringed at her father's use of "beast" to

describe Canna. But the dragon ignored the word. "I do. Dragons are able to choose or reject the Lord, the same as men do. I follow Him." Her white scales shimmered in the sun. Canna almost glowed in the beaming sunlight.

Father bowed to Canna. "Then I apologize for my misunderstanding. Tell me, Canna, why do you want to take my daughter into danger?"

Canna hesitated. "I know of no 'danger' on this trip. Curves, my fellow dragon and friend, says there is trouble, although he does not say what kind. He is concerned about something and wishes for me to join him soon, although it not urgent I hurry there. Beyond that, he is not able to tell me much. At times, there are limits to our being able to communicate mind to mind. This appears to be one of those. He cannot tell me clearly what is wrong."

"I see." Father lowered his eyes and stared at the ground. He kicked his boot against a stone that lay imbedded in the dirt.

Gentry tapped her foot. "Father, I want to go. Canna helped me. She saved my life when the trader wanted to kidnap me. I'm her rider. That means we're bonded. I have to go. I just have to." She breathed in and said strongly, "I want to go."

Father held her eyes. "And if I say no? Will you accept that and not hold it against me for the rest of your life?"

Gentry looked at her feet. She knew the 'right'

answer. But also knew her heart. She chewed her lip, then looked up at her father. "My head would. But my heart wouldn't. The same as if you told me to marry Brody Swansworth. I would say yes, but my heart would never be in it." She held her head high, almost in defiance.

Father nodded once. He stared at Canna. "And what will you do if I say no? Take her anyway?"

"My allegiance is to the Lord of Heaven and Earth. If you say no, I will honor that because you are her father." Canna dipped her head to Father. Her face remained without emotion.

Gentry tried again. "Father, I want to go." She took his hand and held it. "Just this trip. One trip with Canna. Curves said he needed help. We can help. Please. Just this one trip."

Father shook his head but sighed. "Oh, my child. Yes, you can go. But only this one trip." He hugged her tightly. Father looked sternly at Canna. "Will you promise to keep her safe?"

Canna's tone was even. "I promise to do all in my power to keep her safe. But it is the Master Who will protect her in the end."

Father cocked his head. "You speak the truth. It is up to Him." Father looked at Gentry, then sighed. "When will you leave?"

Gentry turned to Canna for an answer. Canna scratched her chin with her front claw. "We should leave soon. As soon as Gentry can say goodbye to her mother. It is a two-day flight to where Curves is."

Father stared from Canna to Gentry. He said, "Then let's go tell your mother. She waits for us at the cliffs." He shook his head. "She suspected that was why you wanted me to talk with Canna. I think she's packed you a lunch." He put his arm around Gentry's shoulders.

Gentry hugged her father and turned to Canna with excitement. "I'll be back soon. Don't leave without me."

Canna smiled. "I will be here, little one."

Gentry and her father headed home.

The girl said her goodbyes, gathered food supplies for the trip, then rushed back to meet up with Canna. As she packed her special things from the first trip, she asked, "You said the Master will protect me. What does he have to say about this trip? Did you have to get his permission to go?"

"He has allowed me to decide for myself whether I will go or not. He will be with me whatever I decide."

Gentry sat down against the dragon's round stomach. "What is Curves saying about what kind of trouble he is in?"

"Mostly he's not. Except to say he's not the only dragon in trouble. I sense there are many others in trouble as well. But over the distance, it is hard to be clear. After his last message, I'm beginning to think this is not wise."

"You mean this could be bad?" Gentry was suddenly cautious. She shook off the doubts. The girl would go. She had her parents' permission, and that was all that mattered.

"Yes, it could be. You should think very hard about whether you will come with me or not. And ask the Creator what He wants you to do."

"You said he would let you decide."

"But I asked Him, first. That's the difference. You need to ask Him before you decide."

Gentry scowled. "Fine. I'll ask him. But I'm still going to make up my own mind."

Canna huffed, and smoke came from her nostrils. "If He says no?"

Gentry straightened her back. "I'll worry about that after I talk to him." She shifted her weight to get more comfortable, then closed her eyes. "I want to go on this trip with Canna. Will you please be with us? And keep us safe?"

The girl could see Canna was not happy with her prayer, but Gentry didn't care. She'd prayed, and that was what mattered. She didn't expect an answer, anyhow.

A powerful feeling came over her. Her eyes widened as she was enveloped in a cloud of light. She didn't hear any words, but she knew—she *knew*—the Creator of all things did not want her to go. But he would allow her to make up her own mind. Danger would follow. Things could go very wrong. But it was for Gentry to decide.

The light faded. Gentry stared at the ground. She shivered. The girl looked into Canna's eyes. "He says I shouldn't go." She swallowed hard. "He didn't say I couldn't go, only I shouldn't go. That's not the same thing. So, I'm going."

Canna fell silent. The dragon closed her eyes. She bowed her head. Gentry watched, knowing Canna was talking to him about her. Finally, the dragon opened her eyes and sighed. "I will take you. He says you are to be allowed to make your own decision. But it may be at great cost."

Gentry crossed her arms over her chest. "But he'll be with us. You say he's always with us. And he'll protect us."

Canna didn't answer. She stared out of the cave. Her voice sounded far away as she replied, "He will be with us. Always."

Gentry nodded. "That's all that counts." She changed the subject. "How long do you think we'll be gone?"

"I can't say. We have food to get us there. We will supply the return trip when we are ready to come back."

Gentry rehearsed the list in her head. She thought about their travels to now and what worked. The girl had brought enough to keep from having to eat fish. Even dried, fish was not her favorite. And killing them…she couldn't get used to the idea. Even if Canna thumped them first.

"Is it cold where we're going?"

"No. You will require only a light tunic and leggings for riding. I will provide all the warmth you will need."

Gentry smiled. "You always do, Canna. You're the best."

"We will see what you believe when we meet with Curves." Canna's tone sounded dry.

Gentry tilted her head. "Why would that change anything?"

"It is said a person may be judged by the friends they keep. You may find some of mine less than admirable."

The girl's eyes flared. "What are you talking about?"

"You will see." Gentry shook her head. Why was the dragon being this somber? Did Canna not want her to come? But the Master had said it was up to Gentry. Very well, he didn't say it exactly. But he did agree in the end.

What did he say, exactly?

He didn't want Gentry to go. He would allow it but not desire it.

But he said I could go if I wanted to. And I want to.

Even if it brought trouble?

What trouble can there be if he goes with us?

She'd almost been kidnapped.

But I wasn't. He protected me. He'll protect me again. He said he would. He always protects his children.

Gentry shut down any further arguments. She was going. Let the trouble come.

* * *

Gentry strapped her pack to Canna's harness. It should be safe from anything the dragon would do, short of diving into the water. If that happened, Gentry had more to worry about than her supplies.

Dragon and girl left at moonrise. As they rose into the sky, Gentry noticed torchlight on the riverbank. She leaned forward and tapped Canna's neck. "Did you see that?"

Canna nodded. "I smelled men this morning. Trelove and Francis Miller are back searching the caves. It is good we left when we did."

Gentry shuddered. "What would have happened if they found you?"

Canna's voice was hard. "Finding me and doing something about me are two very different activities. I will not be cut into pieces easily."

The girl shuddered again. "I don't like them."

The dragon chuckled. "I am not fond of them either. We must be careful when we are at home."

Gentry asked, "So you are staying with me?"

Canna shrugged. "It would appear we can be close to your parents for now. I will remain outside the village until others are as accepting as your mother and father. But we will be watchful in the meantime."

Gentry hugged Canna's neck a bit tighter.

They flew north most of the night. Canna pointed to the sky. "The Dog Star, or the North Star, as it's called. We use it to know how to get where we're going."

The girl watched. "But how do you know which one it is? There are so many…too many to count."

Canna smiled. "Some are brighter, some are different colors. When you study the heavens, you learn to tell them apart." They flew on under the canopy of light.

* * *

They camped the first day after sunrise. The land over which they flew was empty of people. Wooded and crisscrossed with rivers and streams. Low hills rolled along the water. Everywhere was lush and green.

They stopped by a lake for Canna to rest her wings. Gentry got out the figs she'd packed and tossed them one by one into Canna's open mouth. The dragon smacked her lips and rolled in pleasure at the juicy treats.

Gentry laughed. "You look silly."

Canna shrugged. "No one is here to see us. I can't say it matters what others might think. I'll roll if I please." And she did. She ended her roll belly up, her feet in the air. The dragon spread her wings slightly to maintain her balance on her back. Canna laid her head upside down and closed her eyes. "Sleep, little one. I'll wake you when it's time for us to leave."

Gentry helped herself to a piece of cheese. She broke off a large hunk from the block she'd brought. After she'd eaten it, the girl went down to the lake for a drink of water. She dipped her toes in the cool liquid beauty. This was glori—

A sudden splash startled the girl. Gentry jumped back. A large head snapped at her foot, missing it by inches. Gentry shrieked. A snapping turtle the size of Canna's middle came out of the water at her. The girl backed away as fast as she could, but the turtle continued to pursue her. It was faster on land than Gentry could have imagined. The girl screamed again. The turtle snapped at her, missing by less inches than before.

Canna jumped to Gentry's side, lifted the turtle with her head, and flung it back into the air. The turtle turned flips and splashed down in the center of the lake. It disappeared beneath the water, a wake following behind as the monster swam away.

Gentry's eyes were moon sized. "That thing tried to bite me!"

Canna shrugged. "Not everything is as even-tempered as I. You disturbed his rest."

"I disturbed him? I think he wanted to eat me." Gentry shook with both fear and anger.

The dragon settled back down to rest. "Your toes probably looked like little fish. Turtles must eat, too. He couldn't help it if you looked like a snack."

Gentry settled down close to Canna. "What else is out here that will try to have me for breakfast?"

"Nothing as long as you stay beside me. Wake me before you go anywhere."

The girl scowled. "I'm going over by the bushes for a moment."

"Do not step in the poison ivy." Canna closed her eyes and began breathing long, slow breaths.

Gentry picked her way around the bushes, careful not to disturb the poison ivy wound around the trunks of the bushes. She'd had a run-in with the weed before and scratched and itched for days. Gentry did her business and wondered about washing her hands. Afraid to go near the water again, she rubbed her fingers in the dirt to cleanse them of anything that might resemble poison ivy. Better dirty hands than oil from the plants. She returned to Canna's side and lay down beside the dragon. Canna's snores put Gentry to sleep in no time.

But her dreams were uncomfortable and dark. Fierce dragons attacked Canna. She was alone in the air, fighting for her life. Dragons on the ground laughed and mocked at her. Others screeched in fury. Canna's left wing hung down, torn and ragged. The night sky was lit with flames from burning buildings. Everything was being destroyed.

And Gentry had the terrible feeling it was all her fault.

* * *

CHAPTER EIGHT

Canna woke Gentry when the sun was highest in the sky. "Wake, Gentry. We're safe enough to fly this afternoon. We'll rest at night like normal people."

Gentry stretched then looked at the lake. "Do you think it will be safe for me to get a drink? I won't get attacked by that giant turtle, will I?"

"I'll talk to him." Canna stuck her head under the water. Her mouth and nose disappeared. Her eyes werc the last to submerge. Bubbles boiled on the surface as Canna either exhaled or spoke. Gentry couldn't be sure which. Either way, the bubbles popped as they reached the top. After a few moments, Canna's eyes reappeared. She raised her head and let the water run off her chin. "He says you're safe if you don't stay too long."

Gentry's eyes narrowed. "How long is too long?"

"Turtles live hundreds of years. You would be

old and wrinkled before you would be in danger."

"He moved fast enough when he was chasing me."

Canna nodded. "But this time he knows there is a dragon waiting above the waterline. A hungry dragon. Who wouldn't mind turtle for lunch."

Gentry grinned. "Did you tell him that?"

Canna shrugged. "I may have mentioned it. All of it is true, mind you. I am a dragon, I am hungry, and I don't mind turtle. I wouldn't eat someone I'd talked to, but he doesn't need to know that."

Gentry hugged Canna around the neck and ran to the lake. She had a long drink. The girl rushed through a quick bath, rinsed out her tunic and leggings and put on fresh clothing. She laid her wet clothes out on the rocks to dry. Gentry dug in her pack and pulled out some cheese and crackers, along with beef jerky to chew on. She tossed figs to Canna while she ate. Canna lay flat on the grass and accepted the treats as Gentry threw them to the dragon. Canna smacked her lips and drooled a little as she chewed each of the dark purple delights.

Once both appetites were satisfied, and Gentry's clothes were dry (with a little help from Canna's breath) the two cleaned the camping area, packed their belongings, and set off into the sky again.

It was delightful to fly during the day. The sun was warm and became hot, but the breeze off Canna's wings kept Gentry cool. The girl watched deer and elk and mountain lions and sheep all meander below her. Canna flew well above the treetops. Gentry had no idea the world was as big as it was. The hills and mountains went on forever, it seemed. In her forested world, she could see only the next tree line. If she climbed the trees, she might see a distant set of hills, but never far. This…this view of the open was amazing.

Gentry leaned in to ask Canna, "How big is the world, Canna? Could you fly all the way around it? How long would it take?"

Canna turned around and looked at the girl. "No, I cannot. There are oceans…great expanses of water, bigger than the biggest lake you've ever seen. I can't fly across them. They are so wide and so deep the dragon who attempts it would tire of flying and drown."

Gentry's eyes widened. "Really? How is it possible there are oceans? It would have to rain for years to fill a lake big enough you couldn't fly across it."

"They aren't fed by rain, little one. The Master created the world and saw fit to create and fill oceans and seas."

Gentry considered the idea of an ocean and couldn't imagine it. "Could you fly around it?"

"The oceans surround the dry land. We live on islands in the water. They are not close enough to fly from one to another." Canna turned her head forward again.

Gentry shuddered. Her world an island in the middle of water? "How do you know all this, Canna? Have you ever seen the ocean?"

"Yes. You will tomorrow. We will fly along it to where Curves is living. As for how I know, we dragons were given knowledge of much your people have yet to learn." Before Gentry could ask, Canna continued, "I do not know why it is, little one. I know it as a fact, not why it was deemed so."

The girl crossed her arms over her chest. "That's not fair. We should all know the same things."

"Why?"

"Huh?"

"Why should we all know the same? Do you have a need to know all the secrets the Master holds?"

Gentry shifted in her seat. "Maybe not. But it would be nice if we did."

"You would be Him. Can you act with His wisdom and justice and mercy?"

That was a different matter. Knowing what the Creator knew would be good. But acting like him? Being like him? That would be hard.

"Tell me what he's like."

"When you meet Him, you will see for yourself. He is Love. He is Joy. He is Peace. Patience. Gentleness. Goodness. Faith. Kindness. Self-control. He's not full of these qualities. He *is* this. He is the perfect Father, the perfect Friend, the perfect Companion. He is perfect. He is Grace and Glory. Mercy. Truth. I could go on and on…and I usually do." Canna smiled. "I love Him, and He loves me. He loves you, too."

"Did he teach you all that?"

"I learned it from being with Him, and from hearing His Book. The one you keep at your home. The one your father reads to you. I listened sometimes at night."

Gentry nodded. "I know which book you mean. I've never read it. Father used to read it to me at bedtime. He says I'm old enough to read it on my own now. I haven't started."

"When you do, you will learn much about our Maker. But knowing about Him and knowing Him are different."

The girl nodded. She didn't understand it all, but she had the feeling Canna wouldn't be able to explain it in a simple way. Once Canna got started talking about the Master, she never quit. As they flew, Gentry thought over what she knew of the Master. Certainly, he was Lord of Creation. Canna said he was with her always. But was he really? It seemed impossible. Yes, Gentry asked him for things when Canna told her to. And yes, he'd answered the girl. But did that mean he always would? Gentry didn't know. Canna said he loved Gentry. How could he? The girl had her doubts. And she would hold on to them. At least a little longer.

They flew on until the sun dipped below the trees. Canna angled her flight toward an open area that would allow her to land. It was a gentle hill with no trees at the top, with a clear stream running at the bottom. The dragon set her feet on the ground with a thump. Gentry and her pack tumbled forward and landed in the soft grass.

Canna laughed, but with embarrassment. "I am sorry, little one. I've been flying for so long today, I forgot how to land properly. I'll practice tomorrow."

Gentry stood and brushed herself off. "No harm done. I'm fine." She opened the supply pack and made sure everything was still intact. The crackers were still in one piece, as were the figs. No mush. The cheese was smushed on one edge but would still be able to be eaten. All in all, no damage done.

Canna directed, "Gather some firewood as you are going to the creek. I'll wait for you here."

Gentry laughed. "I'm sure you will. You'd never fit between these trees."

Canna huffed. "I could make a path if I wanted to. But the trees are pretty, and I don't want to hurt them."

Gentry smiled and walked down to the stream. The water was cool, almost cold, and tasted wonderful. Canna called, "You should fill your water pouch. When we reach the ocean, you won't be able to drink the water. It's full of salt."

"Salt water? Why can't I drink it?"

"The salt will only make you thirsty. You drink and drink but never quench your thirst. In the end, you will die, surrounded by water you can't have."

"That's horrible. Why would the Creator…" Gentry let the matter go. There was so much about his ways she didn't understand. But Canna would say he had his reasons. The girl filled her water pouch, drank some more from the creek, and climbed the hill back to where Canna waited. She picked up dead tree limbs along the way until she'd filled her arms. She piled them into a mound.

Canna hollowed out a space to place the wood where it wouldn't catch anything else on fire. The dragon lit the logs, and soon they had a cozy blaze. Gentry hauled out the dried food again, but Canna declined. "You keep it. I will hunt meat." She admitted, "I need more protein than the cheese will give me. Flying is taxing work. Not hard, but I burn energy. I need to replace it. I will hunt and eat after you sleep. You will be safe here. I won't leave you alone for long."

Gentry frowned but had to agree. Canna knew her needs. And Gentry had to admit, she'd never heard of a dragon who didn't eat meat. As long as Canna didn't eat people. And the dragon promised she'd never done it and never would. Something more the Creator had decreed.

The sun went down below the trees, and

darkness crept in to fill the land except where the fire burned. Only the stars gave their light. The moon had yet to show its face. It would only be a partial moon as it was.

Gentry curled into a ball, using her pack for a pillow. Canna's belly would have been more comfortable, but the dragon needed to leave. Gentry closed her eyes and muttered, "Good night, Canna. I'll see you in the morning."

"We will arrive to meet with Curves tomorrow. Most likely past noon. I'll be back here before the moon rises. Sleep well, little one."

Gentry was sure she would stay awake until the dragon returned, but she drifted off.

Only to dream the same horrible dream. Canna was injured, being chased by enormous, enraged dragons who wanted to kill her. Gentry stood on a hill watching, unable to do anything to help her friend. An orange dragon soared over the girl's head, its jaws red with blood. It taunted her. "Stupid girl! Thinks she can tame a dragon! Ride a dragon? Not in our lifetime. We'll kill your Canna, then kill you. She can't protect you forever. You should never have come."

The dragon swooped down. Its claws extended to tear Gentry to shreds. She tried to run, but her feet wouldn't move. They seemed frozen to the ground. She screamed, "Canna!"

Canna banked her flight to come to her aid, only

to be struck down by the talons of a mottled dragon. It screeched and shrieked and cried in victory. Canna crashed to the ground, unable to fight back. The host of dragons landed around Canna, mocking and cackling. All of them had their mouths open, waiting for some signal to begin the feast.

A blue dragon with white claws swooped down and picked up Gentry. It dangled her in the air, then dropped her on top of Canna's lifeless body. Gentry landed hard, knocking the breath out of her. All the dragons screamed. They attacked her from all sides…

Gentry jerked awake. Tears streamed down her face. Her heart raced. Her hands shook. Canna was nowhere to be seen. "It was a dream. A bad dream. It wasn't real. It wasn't. It's not my fault. It's not."

The tears wouldn't stop flowing. And the ache in her heart wouldn't go away. Try as she might, the feeling of dread remained. The girl wrapped her arms around her shoulders and buried her head in them. Gentry wept and wept until she had no more tears. And she wept some more.

A swoosh of air, and Canna returned. The dragon landed beside Gentry, smacking her lips and looking well-pleased. "That was delightful." Canna looked in Gentry's face and lost her joy. "What happened, little one? Why are you crying?"

Gentry grabbed Canna around her middle and shuddered. She couldn't stop hiccupping and couldn't explain. It was too awful.

It took several minutes of Canna humming and crooning before Gentry pulled herself under control. The girl wiped her face on her tunic. Gentry let the music calm her spirit as she rested her head on the dragon's belly. She sat at Canna's feet and nodded. "I'm okay now. It was a dream."

Canna eyed the girl, concern in her face. "It must have been a terrible dream."

"It was. You were being attacked by other dragons. They…they knocked you out of the sky. I think they killed you."

Canna's eye ridges rose. "They did, now? Well, that is a terrible dream."

Gentry lowered her eyes. "The worst part was it was my fault." She looked at Canna. "An orange dragon kept saying it was my fault. If I hadn't come, none of it would have happened."

Canna hummed softly. "I see. An orange dragon, you say. Did he have but one eye?"

Gentry shook her head. "I don't know. I don't remember. But he was terrible. And there was a blue dragon with white claws…and a yellow and black one and even a purple dragon."

Canna didn't comment. She shifted her weight, curled around Gentry, and wrapped her tail around her body. "Dreams can be horrible. They can be your mind working out a problem. Or when you're feeling responsible about something, your dreams can play on your guilt."

The dragon paused. "They can also be a warning from the Master." She fell silent. "But those are rare. Most of the time, it's your mind playing tricks on you. Are you feeling like you shouldn't be here?"

"That's just it." Gentry tried to put her feelings in order. "I want to be here. I was told I could be here. That's why I came. But…but it's the second time I've had this dream. The dream keeps telling me it's my fault. If I hadn't come, it wouldn't happen." She stopped, swallowed hard, then admitted, "You wouldn't have died."

Canna hummed again. "I have no intention of dying. I have had no such dreams. I believe your mind is working overtime on you about your guilt. You will have to square it with your mind, Gentry. The dreams will stop. But now, you need to sleep, as do I. I need to rest for the final push to reach Curves and be able to help him with his problem."

"You weren't gone very long. How did you have time to eat?"

"Dragons have special stomachs. We can fill ourselves to the full and eat some more if we have to. The Creator knew I couldn't leave you alone for long, so He allowed me to find and eat my meal with a haste that would make many ill. Or leave them bursting so they could not fly."

"But he made it different for you? Why?"

"He knows. We don't question. We obey."

"But not all dragons follow him." Gentry remembered the conversation they'd had before.

"That is true." Canna smiled. "The good ones do. Curves is one of the good ones. It will be wonderful to see him again."

"Has he spoken to you recently? Told you what is happening?"

"No. He only says I will know when I arrive." Canna lowered her head to the ground. "It is time for sleep, little one. Have sweet dreams. Rest and be ready to fly in the morning."

Gentry leaned against Canna. The warmth of the dragon's belly, the comfort of her tail wrapped around her, made the girl know she would have only good dreams. No more guilt. No more worrying about Canna dying. Just dreams of peace. She slept.

And the nightmares returned.

* * *

CHAPTER NINE

Morning came. At dawn they flew west until Gentry spied a large lake. But the closer Canna flew, the more Gentry realized it wasn't a big lake. It was beyond the biggest lake she'd ever seen. Wild waves crashed against the rocky shore. The blue of the sky came down to meet the blue of the water until you could not tell one from the other. Gentry's eyes widened in awe. She whispered, "Is that the ocean?"

"Yes, little one."

The waves bore white tops that danced in a breeze off the waters. The smell of salt permeated the air. Birds cried and dived and circled and argued. They gave Canna plenty of room but filled the sky with their squawking.

Out beyond where the waves curled and crashed, dark shapes dived and rose above the water. Fish —the biggest fish Gentry had ever seen — frolicked. One rose out of the water, climbing higher and higher…then smashed down on its side with a resounding "boom." It was like nothing Gentry had ever heard before. Her jaw fell open, but there were no words.

Canna smiled at her. "The ocean. One of the Creator's greatest gifts to us."

Gentry couldn't speak. She could only stare out wide-eyed, trying to take in the beauty and majesty.

They flew along the edge of the water, what Canna called, "the coast," for another two hours before Canna circled a clearing between stark ridges of towering cliffs. Rocky and barren, they reminded Gentry of a fortress. She had never seen one, but her father told her tales from his time in the capital, where the King of the land lived. Father had visited the castle once, long before Gentry was born.

Now, looking at the walls of stone, Gentry could imagine what her father had been trying to describe. Tall…tall, tall. The cliffs reached up hundreds of feet until they blocked out the sun. Indeed, all the land remained in shadow except where a strip of sunlight dared to shine.

Wooden structures dotted the area. Gentry asked, "Houses? Do people live here?"

"Once. Not now. This is the birthing ground for dragons. Mothers lay their eggs in the caves in the cliffs. We keep the houses for the young dragons who can't fly back to the caves in the hills. Sometimes a first flight doesn't go as planned, and the younglings must spend the night on the ground. It is usually a new dragon mother who hasn't properly judged her fledgling's readiness to fly. The dragonette will fly down but not be able to fly back up."

Gentry laughed. "Does it happen often?"

Canna shrugged as she glided in for a landing. "Not often. We don't have as many new mothers as we did before. Before we were hunted and our numbers decreased."

Gentry lost her laughter. People hunting dragons. Like Trelove and Francis Miller. Why did she have to think about those two on this trip? This was supposed to be a fun time. A time to help the mysterious Curves.

A thought bothered Gentry. "Canna, what happened to your mother? Why did I find you by the river? You weren't really a baby dragon, though."

Canna nodded on her long neck. "I was a throwaway. Not a proper dragon. My wings didn't form until after I was hatched. My mother thought I would never be a real dragon, so she left me by the river. She hoped I would find a life as a lizard and be happy."

"She flew off and left you? And didn't ever come back to see if you were alive? That's terrible."

"That's a human thought. It's not how dragons live. A deformed dragon is not accepted among us. It wasn't until I grew my wings that the other dragons would let me join them."

Gentry scowled. "That's still terrible."

Canna's tone was soft. "You do not have people who are different than others among you?"

"Well, yeah, we do. Sometimes."

"And are they always accepted by everyone? By you?"

Gentry remembered a boy with only one arm. He'd come through on a wagon with a group of traders. People had gawked at him, and the children wouldn't play with him. Gentry had even been shy of him. The memory made her feel ashamed. She admitted, "No, I guess they're not. But it's wrong to do. I see it now. I should have treated him like he was anyone else."

"Perhaps next time you meet someone different, you will. It is how the Creator wants us to treat all His creations. He loves us all. He wants us to love others the same."

Gentry stared at the ground. "That's hard, Canna. I'd have to love Francis Miller."

"Yes, you would. You don't have to love what he does, but you are to love the man."

"I don't know how to do it."

"If you follow the Creator, you will learn. It's not something we can do on our own. Only with His help."

"Maybe I'll understand some day."

"I'm sure you will." Canna strained her neck to look around the area. She called, "Curves! We have arrived."

The flutter of wings came from overhead. Gentry looked to see a green and yellow dragon floating down from the sky overhead. His body was jewel green, his belly and talons yellow like the sun. He shone in the shadows like a beacon fire glowing in the night. He landed feet from Canna, talons tearing the ground in long strips. The dragon skidded to a stop in front of Canna, who towered over the newcomer.

"Canna," the dragon croaked with a hoarse voice. "It is good to see you again. Who is this you have brought here?"

"Curves. This is Gentry." Canna humped her back so Gentry would climb down.

The girl stepped in front of Curves and froze. How should she greet another dragon? Bow? Curtsey? Kneel? Gentry chose to bow her head in respect. "Sir. It is my pleasure to meet you at last. Canna has had good things to say about you."

"If she has, she's lied." Curves smiled, and his eyes narrowed. "What have you been telling this child, Canna? You know better than that."

Canna laughed. "Only you taught me all I know about flying. And what a talented and skilled flier you are. And you serve the Master."

Curves shrugged. "Well, I suppose those parts are true."

Now that Gentry could see Curves close up, she realized the dragon was showing his age. Though his scales were green, they were tinged in gray at the tips. His face bore wrinkles and scars of many battles. Did dragons fight? Her dream came back to her, and the girl shuddered.

Gentry stepped back to stay out of Canna's way, in case Canna wanted to greet Curves in some way only dragons knew. But Canna sat on her haunches and asked, "Why did you send for me, Curves? You said I would see when I arrived. I see nothing but the fledgling grounds."

"Do you see fledglings? Do you see mothers training them?"

Canna craned her neck to look at the cliffs. After a few moments, she looked back at Curves. "No. Where have they gone?"

"I don't know. I came here seven days ago. I have been searching all along the canyon and found nothing. No sign of anyone, and no way to know where they might be. Nor even how many are missing."

Canna's eyes narrowed. "How long have you been away?"

"Nine months. Twelve at most. There were at least twenty mothers and fledglings. To find this place deserted…something must have happened."

Canna closed her eyes and grew silent. Gentry guessed she was reaching out to the other dragons with her mind, trying to contact them. She opened her eyes finally. "I can hear nothing. No chatter. No talking. No one answers."

Curves nodded. "That is as I have found. There is nothing. As if they didn't exist."

Canna's voice was quiet. "Or ceased to be." The dragon launched into the air, leaving Gentry behind. The girl watched as Canna began flying in and out of the canyon walls, as if searching the caves.

Curves shook his head. "She will find nothing. I have already been over these walls. Everything is empty."

Canna flew to join the two on the ground. She glided in and landed without leaving a mark. She studied Curves.

"How far have you searched up the river?"

"Not far yet." He sighed slightly. "I am not the young dragon I was. I can still handle the canyons, but the heights are a trial."

Canna nuzzled Curves with her head. "You will always be young, my friend. I will see what I can find." She turned to Gentry. "You can stay with Curves. I will be flying where it is too cold for you to go."

Gentry shook her head. "I want to go with you."

"You would be frozen in no time. No, you must stay here."

"But what if you run into trouble? Who will be there to help you?"

"I will be back. If not, Curves can take you home."

Gentry's head snapped up. "He knows where I live?" She glanced to study the jewel green dragon again.

"You can tell him. He's traveled through most of this country. He will know." Canna smiled at Curves.

Curves smiled back and nodded. "I can find any place you can describe." He lifted his chin with some pride.

Gentry held back her tears. She hugged Canna around the dragon's middle. "I love you, Canna. You have to come back. Promise me you will."

Canna repeated, "If the Master allows, I will be back. In the meantime, share your provisions with Curves. I suspect he's not eaten in days." Canna leaned forward and whispered loud enough for Curves to hear, "But not the figs. Save those."

Curves head came up. "Figs? You have figs?" His eyes narrowed, and he leaned in closer.

"Did I say that?" Canna pretended innocence. "Maybe if you're really nice to Gentry, she'll share."

Canna stepped away from Gentry and tucked her wings tight to her body. She stared at the sky, then called, "As You will."

She took a running start, then flapped her wings. The dragon rose from the ground a foot, two feet, and pulled almost straight into the air. In moments she was over the top of the ridge and gone from sight.

Gentry pulled out her bag of food and dug for

the figs. She found them, still ripe and sound. Curves sat on the ground like Canna used to…head down, mouth waiting to receive the juicy delights.

As Gentry tossed them to Curves, she asked, "Why do they call you Curves?"

"I used to fly fast and free. I made curves in the air as I passed. There is a canyon on the other side of the pass where I fly that is nothing but bends and twists. There are too many to count. I like to race it as fast as I can. Which is not as fast as I once could, but still faster than most. I know the angles."

"Does anyone else fly it with you?"

Curves laughed. "No one is as fast as I was. That's why they call me Curves."

Gentry thought for a moment. "That's not your real name?"

"My name is Chronos. But I prefer Curves. It suits me better."

"Chronos." Gentry repeated the name in her head. "I like Curves better as well. It tells me something about you."

"It does indeed." Curves chewed a last fig, then sat. "Thank you, young one. Canna said your name is Gentry. Why do they call you that?"

The girl shrugged. "It's what my mother called me when I was born. She never said why. I guess she liked the name."

"It sounds regal. Like royalty."

"Thank you." Gentry looked around at the

houses. They reminded her of the houses she'd seen burning in her dreams. Not exactly the same but close enough to make her uneasy. She nudged the dirt with her foot. "How long has this place been here?"

"Ages and ages. I think people once lived here. That's why the houses were built. But they abandoned it years before we came."

Gentry grew somber. "Have you been hunted? Canna has."

"The only dragons that aren't hunted are across the Divide with the Master. All we here are considered a threat to people and their animals."

Gentry shook her head. "That's not fair. You have a right to live, too."

Curves smiled, but it was a sad smile. "I believe so, as well. Others have a different opinion. It does take a lot to feed a dragon."

Gentry laughed. "I understand. Canna goes into the hills to hunt her food." The girl stopped. "Do you fish? Do you like fish?"

Curves shook his head. "I know Canna is able to swim under the water and catch fish. She's the only dragon I know who can do that. Except for water dragons. Or sea dragons. But Canna seems to be both a land and sea dragon. Which is why she is considered strange among us."

Gentry stared at the ground. "Do you like Canna? Even with her being different?"

"Of course. Oh, it took some getting used to

seeing a pearl white dragon who was as comfortable under the water as in the air. But once I understood her, I learned to appreciate her differences."

Curves stretched his wings. "Would you like to fly the canyon with me? I will show you why they call me Curves." He smiled. "Without speeding, of course."

Gentry smiled. "That would be fun." She dropped her pack. "I'll leave this so Canna knows we're coming back."

"We won't be gone long. Long enough to look, not long enough to miss her return."

"Of course."

Curves bent one knee down so Gentry could step up. It was easier for the girl to mount the smaller dragon than pulling herself onto Canna's broad body. Gentry grasped Curves around the neck.

Curves twisted to make himself comfortable. He hopped twice and launched into the air. Two flaps of his jade wings, and he was soaring above the houses. He aimed down the canyon and banked to enter the barely visible opening. Gentry held her breath, positive they would crash into the walls. But the dragon wound his way through rock formations with the skill that won him his preferred name. He curled around sharp corners, flying straight up—or down— with total ease.

Easy for him. Breathtaking for Gentry. The girl squealed and giggled as they flew along. Curves ordered, "Hang on." Gentry grabbed tighter to the dragon's neck and squeezed her eyes shut. Whatever was coming, she didn't want to see it.

But her stomach lurched as she sensed they were falling…falling…falling…suddenly Curves opened his wings, and they were soaring again. Straight up. Over the top, down…up…down… Gentry swallowed hard to keep from losing her last meal.

The girl felt the powerful thrust of air as Curves winged backward and slowed his descent. He glided into a smooth and soft landing, barely kissing the dirt with his feet.

Gentry slid off and began laughing. She hugged Curves and smiled. "That was amazing. I've never flown like that before. Canna is wonderful, but you are fantastic."

Curves beamed. "And I was only at half speed. There was a time I could have gone faster, but you would have fallen off."

"I'm glad you went slow on my account." Gentry walked around in circles, getting the feel of solid earth again. Finally, she plopped onto her seat and leaned against her pack. "Thank you, Curves. I know why they call you that now."

Curves fairly beamed with satisfaction. "Canna tries to keep up, but she's too big to make the tight turns. She's the biggest dragon there is. Another way she is 'special.' She's never stopped growing. Every time I see her, she's bigger."

"Bigger than what?"

A mottled orange dragon slid out of the sky. Gentry gasped. It was the dragon from her dream. The one who had attacked Canna. Another dragon followed the first. This one was blue. Then a yellow one appeared, followed by a purple one. The four dragons surrounded Curves as they landed.

Blood drained from the girl's face. Her stomach dropped. Her heart stopped. Gentry's nightmares stood in front of her. Except this time, she wasn't dreaming. They were real.

* * *

CHAPTER TEN

The mottled orange dragon with one eye walked up to Curves and demanded, "Larger than what? Who are you talking about?"

Curves lifted his chin. He narrowed his eyes. "Canna gets larger every time I see her."

The orange dragon snorted. "That one. She's a freak. Whoever heard of a pearl dragon? That started as a lizard? She's not a real dragon."

The yellow dragon jeered, "Not a real dragon at all. She doesn't belong with us."

Curves eyes narrowed further. He looked at the four newcomers with disdain, then turned to Gentry. "Meet Divot, Sunrun, and Bluven." He nodded to them. "Boys." He turned to the purple dragon. "And girl. This is Mauve."

Gentry nodded her head to each dragon as Curves introduced them. She tried to memorize their names. Divot was mottled orange. One eye was scarred and closed. Sunrun was yellow with black patches on his wings. Bluven was blue with white claws, and Mauve was the purple dragon. The girl wondered, were female dragons rare? Curves talked about the mother dragons but didn't mention father dragons. Gentry decided now was not the time to ask.

Divot seemed to be the main speaker. He lashed his tail and stuck his head into Curves face. "Who is this with you?"

"She came with Canna. Her name is Gentry."

Divot snorted but backed off a step. "Why is she here?"

"Canna must have thought it was important enough to bring her." Curves did not appear intimidated by Divot.

But the orange dragon wasn't so easily put off. "We don't like humans here with our younglings."

Curves pointed with his wing. "Do you see any younglings? Do you see any dragons at all except us?"

For the first time, Divot and the others began to look around. Shock, confusion, and suspicion filled their faces. Divot demanded, "Where is everyone? Where did they all go?"

Curves snorted. "That's why I called Canna here to help me find out. There's no one here."

Divot ordered the others, "Spread out. Search the area." Sunrun, Bluven, and Mauve scattered to examine the caves and houses.

Curves sat on the ground and wrapped his tail

around Gentry. Gentry felt safer surrounded by the dragon. It kept the others—and her nightmares—away. He called, "We've already done that. But go ahead and look."

Divot joined the searchers. While the four newcomers were busy with their backs turned, Canna reappeared. The pearl dragon dropped in from the top of the cliff and soared to a screeching halt at the bottom. She looked exhausted. Her face was thin and drawn. Her wings drooped. One eye was swollen closed.

Gentry untangled herself from Curves' protective care and raced to Canna's side. "Canna! What happened to you? Where are you hurt?"

Canna took a moment to breathe. She rubbed her wounded eye against her front leg. Canna looked around at the other dragons who still scoured the area. She turned to Curves. "When did they arrive?"

"A few moments ago." Curves' eyes took in Canna's condition. "What happened to you?"

"I was in a fight." Canna rested her head on the ground.

Gentry's voice rose an octave. "A fight? With who? Over what?"

Canna rubbed her eye again. "A dragon. Over his territory. He didn't believe me when I assured him I wasn't trying to steal his hunting ground."

Curves' eyes narrowed, and his tone hardened. "What dragon?"

Canna shrugged. "It doesn't matter. Wherever the mothers and younglings went, they did not go over the cliffs. I'll have to search further afield to find a trace of them."

Gentry pressed her arms as far around the pearl dragon as she could reach. "You need to rest, Canna. You can't fly all day like this without taking a break."

Curves' voice softened. "Listen to the girl. She speaks wisdom. Isn't that why the Master sent her?"

Canna held Gentry's eyes. Gentry lowered her head but didn't say anything. Canna nodded. "I will rest. What mood is Divot in?"

"Protective of the young dragons. Of which there are none. I had to point the fact out for him. He obviously hasn't been here in some time, or he would know this."

Canna sighed. "I'll talk to him."

Gentry looked over and said, "Here he comes. They're all coming."

Canna took a deep breath and lifted her head. Gentry watched Divot and the others approach.

Divot's eye widened as he saw Canna. He called across the distance, "Look who dragged in. Who put you in your place?"

Canna waited until the group of newcomers assembled in front of Curves, Gentry, and herself. She eyed Divot with her good eye. "You should see the other guy. I won the fight."

Divot hmphed. "So you say. What are you doing here, Canna? You don't belong in these parts. This isn't your home."

Curves spoke before Canna could. "I asked her to come. When I didn't find the younglings or mothers, I asked her to come help me find them."

"Why didn't you ask us?" Bluven challenged. "We live here."

Curves snapped, "Did you live here when the mothers disappeared? You don't know any more than I do. That's why I asked for outside help."

Divot walked and stepped in front of Canna's face. "And what makes you think you should bring a human child to our nesting grounds? After everything humans have done to us, you bring one of them here."

Canna lifted her shoulders. "She is my bondmate. She saved my life when I was but little. She may have a purpose here."

Sunrun fairly spit out the word. "May. And that's enough to bring her? She's barely a child herself. What good is she?"

"The Master has use for all creatures, Sunrun." Canna did not back up under the yellow dragon's verbal attack.

Bluven mocked, "The Master, the Master. I tire of hearing you talk about him." He scratched in the dirt and threw dust in the air with his back leg.

Canna held Bluven in her good eye but said

nothing more. Bluven backed down after a moment. Canna turned her gaze to Divot. "When were you here last?"

Divot looked in the air. "Six seasons ago."

Gentry counted in her head. A year and a half ago.

"All of you?" Canna searched around the ring of dragons. Gentry stayed tucked against Canna's belly, as much out of view as she could be. She sensed the dragons' dislike of her. She didn't want to give them more reason by saying something less than smart.

The other dragons nodded. Mauve motioned with her wing. "I came in from the west and saw no trouble that way. All the mothers and younglings were quite content and busy."

Bluven nodded. "And I came from the east. There was nothing to show the mothers would leave and take the dragonettes with them."

Sunrun agreed. "All seemed well. Plenty of food, plenty of water. The caves were filled with dragons."

Gentry moved aside so Canna could sit down in comfort. The dragon rested her head on the ground but kept all the others in view of her good eye. "Hunters would have left signs. They would have burned the houses or torn them down to use the logs for fires. There would have been scorch marks where the mothers defended themselves and their young. There is none of that."

Divot growled. "Agreed. They left. But where? And why?"

Gentry looked at the stream that flowed down from the cliffs. She could see another channel where water had flowed but was now a dry gulch. The girl stared at it and thought hard. Finally, she asked, "What if the water dried up?"

Divot snorted. "It flows fine."

"It does now. But look." Gentry pointed to what had been the creek. "Was that where the water came from before?"

Everyone stared at the winding path in the dirt. Mauve's eyes narrowed. "Didn't the water come down from the east?"

Divot's voice sounded far off. "It did."

Bluven launched into the air. He climbed above the cavern walls, struggling with his blue wings against the thinning air to reach the top of the ridge. Those on the valley floor had to strain to see him. He disappeared over the summit and went out of sight.

Gentry turned to Canna. "Where did he go?"

"To explore the source of the water. There is a river at the top of the summit that flows to feed the streams. If it has been stopped, it would explain a great deal."

"Like they left because the water dried up?" Gentry tried not to be bothered by the grim looks of Divot and Sunrun.

Canna lifted her head to nod. "Yes."

Curves scowled. "I was here twelve months ago. There was plenty of water. How could it dry in that time, and there still be water today?"

"If the river shifted, it could dry in a day. These mountains move. A rock fall could have cut the water off." Canna rubbed the base of her chin with her claw.

"And opened it back again?" Divot sneered. "Smart rock fall. I don't believe it. Rock falls do not have minds to change."

Canna huffed. "When Bluven returns, we'll know."

Gentry asked, "Can I get you anything?"

"No, little one. I need rest and food."

Curves added, "And more than figs and cheese. You need meat. I'll hunt you a fat buck and bring it to you."

Gentry swallowed hard but nodded. "Yes, you do." She smiled in spite of her stomach curling at the thought. "The fatter the better."

Mauve eyed Gentry hard. "You are feeding her only cheese and figs?"

Canna answered, "No. I have all the meat I need. And fish. I am well fed." She indicated her lengthy body. "As anyone can see." Mauve's eyes narrowed, and she huffed, but she said nothing.

Curves hopped into the air, winged his way down the canyon, and out of sight. Gentry sat beside Canna and leaned her body against the dragon's.

Canna hummed softly. Gentry recognized it as a tune about the greatness of the Master. The girl wondered if the other dragons knew it. Was Canna hoping to upset them? Or did the pearl dragon not care what the others thought? That didn't seem like Canna.

Maybe Canna needed to remind herself how Creator could do anything he chose…even move a river. His reasons weren't something he needed to explain—not to anyone. One more mystery Gentry would have to accept.

Bluven dived down from the summit. His flight angled straight down, as if he were in a great hurry. Divot watched him and growled under his breath. "Show off. The fool is trying to impress Mauve."

Mauve nodded. "I'm impressed. I'll be more impressed when he pulls up safely."

The small crowd at the base of the canyon held their breath as Bluven plummeted down and down without slowing. Divot muttered, "He's going to crash."

Canna lifted herself into the air. Her giant wings beat the air as she raced to meet Bluven. She swooped under him, meeting him with a heavy thump. The pearl dragon carried him up, then eased them both back to the ground. She bent her legs as she hit the earth to cushion the landing. Bluven rolled off Canna's back and fell unmoving at her feet.

Divot and the others rushed to see what was wrong with the blue dragon. His eyes were closed.

One wing was ripped open and bleeding. Scales fluttered down from the sky, torn from his shoulders.

Divot touched his friend with his nose. He poked him in the chest. He laid his head on his heart to listen.

Gentry held her breath. She whispered, "Please. Please. Let him be alive."

Divot raised his head. "His heart is beating. He's breathing."

Canna moved to stand beside Bluven. She bowed her head and closed her eyes. The pearl dragon fell silent. Gentry thought Canna was praying. Why didn't she heal Bluven like she had William?

The girl remembered what Canna had said, "If the Master wills." Why wouldn't he? If Canna could do all these special things, why wouldn't he let her show her friends what he could do?

Another thing she didn't know about him. And would have to learn. Soon.

Bluven blinked his eyes. He raised his head and looked at the others standing around him. He tried to move his wings but squawked in pain. "It's broken. He broke it."

Divot stepped back. "Who? Who broke your wing?"

Bluven yelled, but didn't use words anyone could understand. Tears flooded from his eyes. Gentry watched as the drops fell from the dragon's face and landed on the ground…as plain water. No stones formed. She stared at Canna in awe and confusion but said nothing. Gentry remembered Canna's words: only great love could cause a dragon to cry and their tears form into precious stones. What great love made Canna sad enough to cry gems?

Canna lifted her head and opened her good eye. "Rest. Don't try to move. Stay still until we can heal your wing."

"Heal it?" Bluven shouted. "It won't heal! You can't heal it. No one can. I'm done for."

Mauve nestled close to the blue dragon. "Don't say that. Don't."

Divot pushed her away. "Who did this? Who did you fight?"

Bluven moved his head side-to-side. "I don't know who it was. I've never seen him before. But he was big, and he was mean, and he attacked me before I could say a word."

Divot looked at Canna. She nodded. "I was over the south cliff, and it happened to me as well. He does not speak. He swoops down from above, no challenge, no warning."

Sunrun asked, "Did you see him coming?"

"No. He came out of the sun. I heard his screech, and I looked up. He was on me before I could prepare." Canna looked at Bluven.

Bluven nodded. "It was the same with me. He's a renegade."

Divot's tone darkened. "I think we know what happened to the mothers and young."

Gentry's eyes widened. "He'd kill his own kind?"

"And humans don't?" Divot sneered.

Gentry stared at the ground. "I thought…I thought dragons were different."

Canna said softly, "We are fallen creatures as you are. It is why we need the Creator to save us. From ourselves, as He does for you. No one else can."

Divot stomped his foot. "You talk about your master. Where is he? Why doesn't he stop this? If he's so good, why doesn't he swoop in and fix all this?"

Gentry remembered her conversation with Canna about that very thing. And Canna's answer. The girl said, "So you could choose your own path. And accept or reject him." Gentry bit her lip but looked at Canna. "I understand."

Divot sneered, "You're a girl. You wouldn't understand any of this."

Canna kept her voice even. "If He did step in, would you believe Him? Would you accept Him? Give Him your life and follow Him?"

Divot laughed, and it was harsh. "He'd never do that."

"If He did, would you?"

"Let him do it, and I'll think about it."

Canna shook her head. "That is not the bargain He offers. You believe, and He acts. Not the other way around." She muttered to Gentry, "Except in very rare times."

Mauve tossed her head. "I don't care about him. I care about the colony of mothers and dragonettes. How could one dragon destroy all of them?"

Bluven ruffled his good wing. "Because he is so large, and so full of hate. He flies on the unsuspecting. Maybe after a few of the mothers or their young were ambushed, the others left. Maybe it was both the cutting off of the water and the dragon himself. I don't know. But I know I don't want to face him again. He's bigger than Canna."

Sunrun eyed Bluven. "How did you escape?"

"He let me go. He attacked me, broke my wing, then released me over the canyon."

Divot's eyes narrowed. "If Canna hadn't caught you, you wouldn't be talking to us."

Mauve walked over in front of Canna and lowered her head to the pearl dragon. "You saved my friend. I owe you."

Bluven added, "That goes for me as well. You saved my life. Thank you."

Canna dipped her head. "You are welcome. I haven't saved anyone. Until we rid this place of the renegade, we are all in danger. What's to say he will allow us out of the canyon? Especially now. He knows he can defeat us one by one."

Divot declared, "We'll fight him together. He can't beat all of us."

Above, high overhead, they heard the screech of the renegade. It sounded very much like eerie laughter. Gentry shuddered. She knew now why the Master said she shouldn't come. Canna would have to fight…and maybe be hurt or die. And Gentry would be left alone in a land she didn't know, with no way home. The girl backed against Canna for warmth and courage. But even with the dragon's belly beside her, Gentry knew—she knew—she was in trouble. And there was no way out.

* * *

CHAPTER ELEVEN

Mauve sidled up to Canna. The purple dragon kept her voice low, but she pleaded, "You can save him. I know you can. The others. They don't believe. But I've seen you. I know you can heal him. Please."

Canna gave Mauve a sad look. "I can heal no one. The Master heals through me. Bluven has to let the Creator make him well."

Mauve's face turned fierce. "I won't let him give up without a fight. He's going to be healed. I won't let him accept defeat like this." She marched over to where Bluven lay, his torn wing stretched to the side of his body.

Gentry couldn't hear the conversation, but the girl saw Mauve point to Canna and shake her angry head in Bluven's face. The purple dragon was animated as she argued and pleaded and demanded and begged Bluven to listen to reason. Or faith...

Before the argument was near over, Curves

returned with two fat moose in his claws. The older dragon flew low to the ground. The weight of the animals slowed him. But he flapped his wings and stayed in the air long enough to reach the gathering of dragons and drop the bucks in their middle. He called, "There. I'll go get another two."

Divot called, "No, wait. That's enough. We have a bigger problem than food."

Curves landed and eyed Divot. "Bigger than food?" He saw Bluven and hopped into the air in surprise. "What happened to him?"

The orange dragon explained, "He was attacked by a renegade dragon at the top of the cliffs. The same one who attacked Canna. We think he might have had something to do with the dragons leaving the valley."

Canna moved away from Gentry. She looked the girl in the eye. "We're going to eat. It won't be pretty. You can go into the nearest house if you need to, so you won't see us."

Gentry started to refuse but changed her mind. She had nothing to prove to anyone. The girl nodded to Canna and walked stiffly to the nearest wooden structure. She would be sheltered enough not to hear or see the dragons tear into the moose for their meals. At least the animals were already dead. She wouldn't have to listen to them breathe their last.

She hummed and sang to herself rather than listen to the dragons feast. She echoed tunes she'd heard from Canna. Songs about the Master and how great he was. Songs praising him for his love. Gentry didn't know all the words, but she knew enough to recognize the themes. The girl finally stopped humming and singing and began talking. "You're the only one who can help us with the bad dragon. I don't want any of the dragons to be hurt. Can you make the bad dragon go away? Leave everyone alone? And bring back the mother dragons and their young ones?"

Gentry bowed her head. "I know you didn't want me to come on this journey. I see how it will be harder on Canna. She needs to fight, but she'll be worried about me, and maybe won't pay attention like she should. I'm sorry I came. Sorry I didn't do what you said."

Tears drained from her eyes. "I did everything wrong. I knew what you wanted and didn't care. I'm as bad as the dragons who won't do what you say. Please, can you fix this? Make it all come out right? Canna says you can do anything. Except make us choose to follow you. You won't make us. I'm sorry I didn't listen. Will you forgive me?"

A white light filled the room where Gentry stood. She sensed a warm presence, like a hug. In her head, she knew she'd been forgiven. But there was something more, something else she needed to add.

The girl nodded. "Yes, I will follow You. I will do what You say. Even if I don't understand it. I will be Your servant."

The light grew into a flash of joy. It blazed bright in the dark room, illuminating all the dark spaces. It lasted for several moments, then disappeared from the building. But it stayed in Gentry's heart. She knew what Canna meant by Him never leaving. He would be with her from now on, no matter what happened. Gentry knew then what love made Canna weep gems. The love of the Master.

Gentry wanted to rush to tell Canna. But a voice in her head stopped her. *I know, little one. I saw the light. I am so happy and proud of you. Now begins your greatest adventure: the adventure of following the Master. We will take it together.*

The girl laughed out loud, and it felt good. After all the fear of the dreams and the uncertainty of the outlaw dragon, this felt wonderful.

She waited until Canna spoke in her head again. *It is safe to return. We have finished the meal.*

Gentry walked back to join the circle of dragons. Bluven looked worse. His wing had stopped bleeding but hung loose and useless. The cut was still jagged. Scales continued to slip off into a puddle at his feet.

Mauve hovered near her wounded friend. The purple dragon was pale from worry. Her normal purple-blue scales had become washed out, almost pink. The dragon constantly looked from Bluven to Canna and back again. As if she expected Canna to do something at any moment. But Canna remained seated by the fire someone had lit.

Divot paced back and forth. "We have to do something about the renegade. We need to drive him out. There's five of us. We should be a match for any dragon, no matter how big he is."

Bluven growled. "Six of us."

Mauve snapped, "You can't fly, much less fight. You're no good to anyone in the air."

Sunrun corrected, "Four. Curves is too old to put up the kind of fight we're going to need."

"I'll be the bait. I will do my part." Curves lifted his head and glared at Sunrun. "I'm still a dragon."

Divot scowled, "Fine. We have four able-bodied dragons and Curves. We should still be enough to bring him down."

Gentry listened as the dragons made their plans. Curves would be the decoy who drew the renegade out of hiding. While he concentrated on Curves, the other four would attack him from all sides. Only after the renegade dragon was defeated could they return to looking for the mothers and fledglings who should be here.

Sunrun scowled. "We need six. One on each side, one above, and one below. Otherwise, he slips through our trap."

Mauve ignored the other dragons. She stood between Bluven and Canna. Her gaze shifted from Bluven to Canna. The faded purple dragon begged. "Please. I know you can heal him."

Canna didn't respond. Gentry started to ask, then stopped. Follow the Master. His will was what mattered. She said silently, *In Your will. Only in Your will.* She didn't want Canna to fight. She didn't want any of the dragons to fight. Canna would know what to do.

Mauve urged Canna, "I've seen you heal others. Please." She kneeled in front of Canna. "I'll do anything. Please."

Canna dropped her eyes and sighed. She stood silent for several moments, looked at Mauve, and nodded.

Mauve nearly fainted in relief. Canna stepped over to Bluven and studied his wing. She looked at the blue dragon and ordered, "Don't move."

Divot snarled, "We don't have time for your games, Canna. If you're not with us, say so. This pretending someone can make dragons better is all a trick. They weren't sick to begin with. Or they weren't as hurt as they made out to be. You can't heal a broken wing. Unless it wasn't broken at the start."

Canna ignored him. She held Mauve's eyes. "Do you believe the Master can do this?"

Mauve lifted her head. She gazed steadily into the pearl dragon's eyes. "Yes. I believe the Master."

Canna ignored the jeers of Divot and Sunrun. She closed her eyes. Her mouth moved for several moments. She inhaled a long breath. As she exhaled, a white cloud surrounded Bluven's wing. It covered the wounds so no one could see them.

Divot and Sunrun fell silent. Their jaws fell open. Sunrun muttered, "There is no way."

Canna let the cloud thin out, breathed out again. Another cloud of vapor covered the wing. Canna stepped back. Gentry remembered William and his healing. Canna was waiting for the mist to disappear.

In the fading of the haze, Gentry began to see the wing. The jagged cut was gone. The wing was covered in scales as it had been when Bluven flew in. He'd been healed.

The blue dragon moved his wing, then moved it again. And again. He flexed it, flapped it, moved it around in a circle. His eyes widened into pie plates. He laughed and crowed and jumped. He shouted, "Thank you! Thank you! I'm healed!"

Mauve fell at Canna's feet. "Thank you. Thank you." Her face bore a look of amazement and awe.

Canna shook her head. "Thank the Creator. He did it. I did nothing but call on His Name. He did all the work."

Mauve's face changed. She grew solemn. She looked from Canna to Bluven. The blue dragon was still dancing and celebrating his new strength. Mauve swallowed hard. She gave Canna a determined look and said, "I will thank Him. I do. From here on out, I serve the Master."

Canna wrapped her neck around Mauve's. She hugged the purple dragon. Mauve's color returned.

She went from her faded-out pink to a rich, royal purple. Her eyes shone with a new light. Her claws radiated beauty. Everything about her changed. She was a new dragon.

Divot and Sunrun gawked. Sunrun stuttered, "That's not possible. None of this is possible."

Gentry shouted, "You saw it! Bluven has his wing healed. You can't deny it. The Master healed him."

Divot snapped, "You don't know. I believe it wasn't broken to begin with. He needed rest." He glanced around at the others and sneered, "We still have to deal with what's up there." He pointed a wing at the top of the cliff.

Gentry turned to Canna and Mauve. The girl reached out and put her hands on both dragons. She looked at Canna, then Mauve, and asked, "What does He want us to do?"

Canna considered the question. She looked at Mauve, who returned her gaze. The two nodded. Canna said, "We should try to talk to the dragon, first. I will go."

Mauve eyed Canna from the side. "Shouldn't you heal yourself first?"

"The Creator has not deemed it necessary. I can fly to the top of the cliff and engage him in conversation. If I fail, I will return, and we will hunt him down."

Divot sneered, "What makes you think you will

return?"

"Even Bluven returned. I will be back."

"You're losing us a hunter." Divot's voice filled with disgust.

Canna stared off to the side. "I have to try. I must offer him terms of peace first."

Gentry hugged Canna. "Please be careful. I'll ask the Master to watch over you."

Canna smiled. "I'll be back. And you will be cared for. That is my promise to you."

Gentry closed her eyes. "You worry about you. Don't think about me. I'll be a distraction. You need to concentrate on what you're doing." She gave the dragon a hug and looked her in the eyes. "I love you, Canna. Trust Him."

Canna smiled, then jumped as high as she could. Her wings flapped, and she began the long climb to the top of the cliffs.

Sunrun jeered, "'I love you, Canna.' Like a human can love a dragon. You're always hunting us."

Gentry started to say something, then stopped. She waited, then said, "It's true some people hunt dragons. But I don't. I wouldn't do anything to hurt you or any of your kind."

Divot snorted. "Yet. You will. You humans always do. Like now. If something happens to Canna, it will be your fault because she's distracted. She can't help but think about you. You made yourself her bondmate. Bondmates think of their partners above all else."

Gentry inhaled while she counted to ten. "Canna thinks only of the Master. He's her true concern."

"And what has he done for her, hmm? Sent her off to be killed by that monster there."

Gentry didn't try to argue with Divot. She sensed it was futile. The girl would let Canna debate with the orange dragon.

Together, Gentry and the five dragons watched Canna fly higher and higher until she reached the top of the ridge. She went out of sight.

A terrifying scream came floating down from the summit. Gentry held her breath. She asked, "Please protect Canna. Please."

Divot sneered, "You may as well ask the wind. You'll get more response."

Mauve burst out, "Stop! You don't know what you're talking about. She's right to ask the Creator. You said if you saw a miracle, you'd believe. You saw one. Where's your word?"

"I didn't see a miracle. Bluven was probably only stunned. His wing was never broken to begin with. I don't care what you say. There is no Master."

Gentry laid her hand on Mauve. "He is free to believe what he wants. The Creator has given him the choice. He's wrong, but that will be for the Master to fix." Or not. She didn't add the last thought. Divot was free to choose.

Bluven slid beside Mauve and Gentry. "I don't care what he says. I know it was broken. And now it's not. I don't know how she did it, but I know it's healed."

Gentry shook her head "It wasn't Canna. She doesn't have any special powers. It was the Master Who healed your wing. You need to thank Him. Canna would tell you the same thing. Thank the Master."

Gentry put her hand on Mauve's shoulder and watched the sky. The screaming from above made her shake. It couldn't be Canna. It couldn't be. But why would the other dragon be crying out? Fear? Pain? Anger? Gentry couldn't tell what the sound meant.

The girl looked at Mauve. "Can you understand anything? Are there dragon words in there?"

Mauve shook her head. "Only anger. Dragons don't have a special language. We speak as you do." She looked Gentry in the eyes. "I hear only hate."

Gentry swallowed hard. She closed her eyes and whispered, "You can do anything. Save Canna. Make them friends. Please. Don't let them fight."

The screaming went on and on. Then it stopped. All went silent. Dragon necks craned to try to see anything they could. But there was nothing. No clue. Gentry held her breath again. Longer this time. Until it hurt and she had to breathe again. What was happening? Where was Canna? Was she alive?

A figure came plummeting from the sky above the cliffs. Another followed, diving faster and faster. No one could tell which dragon was which…or if it was Canna at all.

The dragon nearest the bottom pulled up inches from the canyon floor and soared back into the sky, climbing away again. He was a swirl of brown and black and yellow and red and green and purple…like a kaleidoscope of all colors. He reflected light from his diamond claws. He screamed as he streaked by them.

The second figure was Canna. She, too, pulled up at the last moment and zoomed into the sky. A single white scale dislodged as she went by and floated to the ground. Gentry ran to catch it. She cradled the scale in her hand.

Canna mounted the cliffs again in hot pursuit of the renegade dragon. They soared out of sight again. Curves jumped into the air. "She's not going alone."

Divot hopped and knocked Curves back to the ground. "You can't outfly either of them, old worm. Stay here. I'll go."

Mauve grabbed Divot and held him down. "No. I'm going." She didn't stop to argue. The purple dragon threw herself into the sky, trumpeting her defiance.

Divot took off as well. So did Sunrun. Bluven rose from the ground and tested his new wings. He joined the chase. Which left Curves.

The old dragon gave a fierce cry, "I'm not useless."

Gentry urged him, "Go, Curves. You can do it."

The green dragon ran to get up speed, spread his wings, and rose into the air. He circled the valley to gain height, circled again to gain speed. Finally, he pointed his neck to the sky and headed straight up to join his comrades. He might come late to the fight, but Gentry knew they would fight together.

In moments, the dragons disappeared over the cliff, and Gentry was alone. The girl kneeled in the dirt and did the only thing she could. She prayed. "Please. If it's Your will, save them all. Protect them and make them friends. I know You can do all things. But I know You have Your will. I want Your will, no matter what it is. Because I know You're good, and You're the Creator. You know everything. Have Your way, Master. Have Your way."

Whatever happened, she would accept it. He knew. And He loved. That was all that mattered. A tear fell from her eye. "But if You will, please keep Canna safe. I love her."

She sat to wait.

* * *

CHAPTER TWELVE

Gentry walked around the canyon area, looking in the buildings and houses. She wandered through the stone hearths and walls, looking for something maybe the dragons missed. Maybe someone small would see what someone large didn't. Overhead she could hear cries and screams telling her the battle went on. And on. And on.

An hour of searching left her with no more information than she had before. The dragons and their young were gone. She kicked a rock in the dry riverbed. It uncovered a long furrow in the dirt. Gentry eyed it, curious as to its meaning. If it had a meaning. The girl kicked back a few more rocks. Underneath were more lines. Her eyes flared wide. Gentry began picking rocks and throwing them aside. She swept the area with her tunic, brushing back the dirt and leaves.

Excitement grew in her. The lines went straight in all different directions. She realized she was seeing writing as a dragon would do, tearing at the earth with their talons. Gentry cleared as much as she could before she had to stop. No more lines showed. The girl stepped back and tried to make sense of what she saw. She ran her finger down the shapes. After tracing the tracks for long minutes, she decided the message was best read from the air. But she couldn't fly. She'd have to work it out for herself.

Could she?

She had to. It was too important to leave for later when the dragons returned. If they returned.

Gentry copied the lines, making them smaller. She repeated the directions they went and where they were connected. She wasn't sure she got them all right, but she got enough to make out the word "northeast" and a word that made no sense. Trenzore. What did it mean? Was it where the mother dragons had gone? How could she be sure?

Gentry lowered her head. "Help me. I can't reach Canna, and I'm afraid if I did, I'd only distract her from the fight. Can You tell her what I found? And make her understand if it's important? If it's not, don't bother her. In Your will, please."

She sat down beside the riverbank and waited. Heat in the canyons made it hard to draw a breath. There was no wind. There were no birds, either. There were only the sounds of the battle. And the waiting.

The Creator would act, one way or another. She

was sure of it. She didn't know how He would, but she had confidence in Him. If this were important, the dragons would know.

More time went by. Gentry heard a faint echo in her mind.

Little one. You found something.

Excited, Gentry shouted, "A message!" The girl realized Canna couldn't hear her voice. Gentry tried again, thinking as hard as she could, *Trenzore. Trenzore. Canna, it says Trenzore.*

The voice in her head went silent. Nothing more came. Gentry repeated over and over, *Trenzore. Trenzore. Canna, it says Trenzore.*

Would the dragon understand? Would it mean anything to her? Or to anyone else?

The renegade dragon dove down from the clifftop. He swooshed past Gentry, knocking her down in his haste. He didn't stay but barreled back into the sky. He screamed as he flew.

Canna and her friends made a slower descent, but they, too, flew down, then climbed into the air back above the rocky crags.

There was none of the defiance that marked the beginning of the battle. Canna's powerful wings moved slower than before. Divot bore a deep burn mark on his head. Sunrun had one on his left wing. Mauve struggled to push through the sky. Her wings drooped. But she held her head high. Bluven's healed wing looked strong. His other one sagged. He had scorch marks on his shoulder.

Curves was missing. Gentry's eyes flared as she realized the older dragon wasn't with the others. Had he crashed? Been killed by the renegade? Her heart caught in her throat. "Please. Not Curves. Let him be okay. Oh, I know, I have to ask that it be in Your will. I know Your will is best and right. But if there's any way, can it be Your will Curves be alive? And okay? Please. You're good, and You're full of love for all Your creations. Including Curves." She lowered her head. "I love You. It's up to You."

Curves served the Master. He would be taken care of. One way or another.

Gentry leaned against a boulder and watched the ridge overhead. She could see nothing of the battle, but she continued to peer into the sky. Every so often a shadow would cross the sun, or the canyon, but it was too fast to know if it was a dragon, or a bird, or just a cloud. The day dragged on.

And on and on and on.

At last, Mauve returned to the canyon floor. She breathed heavily, her exhales coming in exhausted puffs. Smoke formed small clouds as she panted her fatigue. The purple dragon collapsed to the ground and lay still.

Gentry ran to her and hugged her belly. "Mauve. Oh, Mauve."

The dragon's eyes were open, but unfocused. She said nothing.

Bluven fluttered down. He, too, bore all the marks of the battle. Tired beyond expression, he lay beside Mauve. He closed his eyes and exhaled a long, heavy sigh.

Sunrun and Divot flew down together. Neither spoke, neither made a sound. The only noise was the flapping of their wings in slow, steady beats that barely caught the air. They stumbled rather than glided into a landing. Both hung their heads and sank down to lie on their backs with their feet in the air. It should have looked comical.

It wasn't.

Last came Canna. She carried Curves on her back, dipping first one way, then another, to keep the older dragon stable. Gentry could see deep cuts on Canna's shoulders and legs. Her claws were worn almost to nubs. The pearl dragon's sheen was gone. She looked thin and worn and weary. She barely moved her wings. But she landed at a run in order not to drop Curves. Only when she had come to a full stop did she tenderly let the green and yellow dragon slide from her back onto the ground. Canna crumpled into a heap.

Gentry walked over to her, too afraid to run. She stepped without making any noise so as not to disturb Canna's rest. The girl tiptoed to the dragon's side and placed a hand on Canna's middle. She stroked the dragon and whispered, "Canna…I love you." There was so much else she wanted to say. But now was not the time. Gentry sat down with her back against Canna's belly and cried. It was all she could do.

The renegade dragon circled the canyon. He circled lower and lower and landed on his four feet some distance from the challengers. His eyes were slits, his teeth bared. His wings sagged, torn in several places. Burns marked over half his face and along his sides. Gentry pulled herself to her feet. She walked out to meet the enemy. The girl had no idea what she would do or how she would face this monster. Her friends had done what they could. Now it was her turn.

The dragon watched her advance. He hissed, "Human. You dare come in this valley?"

Gentry prayed to the Master, then spoke to the dragon. "I came because help was needed. Mothers and younglings were missing. Curves asked for help finding them."

"And did you find them?" It was an accusation.

Gentry admitted, "I think I have. Trenzore. I think they went there."

"And you want me to believe this?"

"I've never heard of Trenzore. I have no way to know where it is. But the scratches in the ground said northeast and Trenzore. I don't know if it's north or it isn't."

"Where did you find this message?" The anger and the distrust pounded in his voice.

Gentry waved over her shoulder. "In the river.

Or what was the river. I moved a rock and found a scrape mark. I moved more, and the message showed up."

The dragon glared at her. "Never trust a human. You lie."

Gentry spoke the words that came to mind. "Don't trust me. Look for yourself. I'm sure you saw the writing when you came down before. I have no way of knowing where anything is in this country. With some help, maybe we can turn up more of the message."

"We?" The dragon fairly screamed his reply. "There is no we. There are only dragons. Dragons you and your kind kill."

Gentry snapped back, "My kind doesn't live here. If they did, it was so long ago no one remembers them. Otherwise, why would dragon mothers feel safe enough to raise their young here? Men might hunt a single dragon, but a colony of dragons? There is no way men could fight mothers protecting their younglings."

Canna lifted her head. Gentry saw and called, "Rest, Canna. I have this."

"You have nothing," the renegade dragon sneered. He meant to march around the girl but stumbled instead. Gentry could tell the fight had taken as much out of him as the others.

Gentry made her tone even. "Have you seen men in these parts? In this country?"

"It doesn't mean they haven't been."

"Are you telling me you would miss seeing and smelling a human? In all this desert, you would not see their fires? Smell the meat they cooked? Sense their very being? You may be many things, but careless is not one of them."

She waited for the dragon to swallow that bit of wisdom. She pushed on. "What is your name? So I can call you something proper. Please."

The dragon rested one of his legs across the other. He stared at Gentry. "Why are you not afraid of me?"

"The Master has given me courage."

"Who is this Master who makes a human child stand with only courage in front of Kammere the Great?" The dragon began pacing in front of the girl.

Gentry lifted her head. No matter what happened, she would make the Creator proud.

I already am, little one.

Gentry wanted to look behind her but didn't. She had to keep her focus on Kammere. "You may be Kammere the Great, and you may be master of what you see. But there is a Creator of all that breathes and all that doesn't. He hung the stars in the sky and tells the sun and moon to shine. He created you and gave you life. He knows you and watches every move you make."

"He watched me defeat your friends!" Kammere ground a path in his strutting back and forth.

"He watched. He knows how you rage against Him. But He will bring you low in His time." Gentry's chest swelled with all the words that filled her. "He knows where you live in the tree lands of Mensch. How you followed the river to look for the dragon colony. You didn't find it. You raised the dust in your anger. It was the dirt that covered the message. You never saw it because of your bluster and fury. You vowed you would destroy any who came here. You were convinced anyone who showed was guilty of driving the colony away. You never asked, you never sought help, you just attacked."

Gentry pointed to her friends, who sat staring at her. Even Curves moved. "They came to help. Came to search. But you tried to destroy those who could have located the colony."

"And how does a human child know all this?" Kammere's tone lost some of its arrogance. But none of his distrust.

"I told you. The Master knows all things. He gives wisdom to His servants."

"He's a human?"

Gentry answered quickly, "No. He is King over all. Humans, dragons, the fish of the sea and the birds of the air, and all the animals in between. He is Master."

Kammere stopped pacing and stared at Gentry. "If you know so much, why did they leave?"

"The river shifted. A landslide blocked it from

flowing down the canyon. There was no water. The dragons had to find a new place for themselves." Gentry's eyes widened as another thought popped in her head. "Your mate, whom you call Pleasance, was chief among those who suggested they leave. She took five dragonettes with her."

Kammere froze. His mouth hung open. His eyes fixed on Gentry. His voice was a whisper as he said, "How do you know her name? A name no one calls her but me?"

Gentry smiled a straight-lipped smile. "The Creator knows everything. He tells His servants what we need to know to show His greatness."

Kammere lowered his head. "He is Master." He stared at the ground. "I have been wrong."

Gentry's voice became soft. "He knows. And He loves you anyhow." She reached out to touch the shimmering renegade…outlaw no more. "He forgives you. Pleasance is waiting. Go to her. The Creator will be with you."

"How will I know what He wants?" Kammere seemed almost frightened, if that were possible from the massive dragon.

Gentry assured him, "He will teach you. There are others who know Him snd will show you the Truth. Canna is one. Curves is another. Mauve is learning, too. Ask and He will be there for you."

Kammere bowed his head again and took off slowly into the sky. He circled the canyon once, crying a farewell, then headed northeast.

Divot climbed to his feet. "You let him go!"

Gentry stared at him. Her jaw dropped. "How was I supposed to keep him here? He's a dragon."

"You impressed him with stuff about the master. You could have made him do anything. Even banished him somewhere."

"Why would I? He was looking for his family. Yeah, he did it all wrong, but he still wanted what you wanted. To find the dragon colony."

"Humans! Never get it right."

Canna pulled herself to her feet. "He didn't kill us. He could have, but he didn't. He is a changed dragon. You'll see. When you join the colony, you'll see a different Kammere. The Master will teach him what he needs to know."

Divot mocked, "Sure, he will. Your creator — magically out of the blue —makes you understand stuff. It's not real."

"No? How did Gentry know the name of Kammere's mate? How did she know there were five dragonettes?"

"It was a trick. You must have told her," Divot huffed.

"I didn't know his name, much less the name of his mate. How could I know he even had a mate?" Canna's voice mirrored her frustration. "Be a fool, Divot. You have the choice. He loves you still."

Bluven rolled to his feet. "I believe you, Canna.

And you, little human. I want to learn more about the Creator."

Sunrun looked from Divot to Canna, back to Divot. The dragon's eyes narrowed. He made his choice. He went to stand beside Divot. "I won't be taken in. I'm with you, Divot."

Curves came to his feet. He shook himself, then ambled over to join Canna. "It is good to have more brothers and sisters in the family. I'm happy to welcome you."

Bluven hung his head. "I'm sorry for the nasty things I said about you."

"Forgiven. How can I hold something against you He has forgiven? That would make me higher than He, and there is noOne higher. I can hold nothing against anyone, because He forgave everything in me." Curves extended his wing to touch Bluven's.

Canna smiled. "This is all good. We should rest, heal, and go check on the colony. Now that Gentry has shown us where it is."

"The Master showed us." Gentry corrected her friend. "I just kicked a rock."

Curves stretched his wings and back. "Too bad you couldn't have kicked it before we fought with Kammere."

"Next time." Gentry laughed.

Canna smiled again. "Indeed. Next time. Next adventure." She asked, "Now, who's up for hunting?"

Everyone groaned.

* * *

EPILOGUE

Three days later, Gentry and Canna arrived home late in the afternoon. Canna circled the caves, then veered off and headed to the river. She sniffed. "Men. Francis Miller and his friend Trelove." She shook her head. "I will put you down closer to your house then find a place to stay."

Gentry growled. "They are a thorn in my side."

Canna laughed. "You're not the one they want to cut into pieces. We will need to teach them a lesson."

"When? How?"

"Excellent questions. I will have to ask the Master about it. I suggest you do the same. Until then, you are to…"

"Obey my parents. Do all the good I can, all the times I can. Learn all the Creator has to teach me." Gentry chuckled. "I know, Canna. I know."

Canna smiled. "You learn fast. The Book will

teach you what you need to know."

Gentry cocked her head. "Mauve and Kammere don't have the Book to read. How will they learn?"

"The Master Himself will teach them. As He did me. You have the advantage of having His Word to read anytime you want. You should be happy for it."

"I am. Or I will be. From now on, I promise." Gentry crossed her heart with her hand.

"That is good, little one." Canna flew to a place upstream from Gentry's house. She found an area large enough for her to land on the river and float to the shore.

Gentry climbed off, landed in the water and trudged through the mud to the shore. She hugged Canna. "I love you, Canna."

"I love you, Gentry. We will go on other adventures, I promise. As soon as your parents will allow. Think about how to rid ourselves of Miller and Trelove."

"I'll be praying about it every night."

Canna reminded her, "And day. We speak with the Master as with a friend. All the time."

Gentry nodded. "Right. I will." She started to her house, stopped, and ducked down. "Hide, Canna!"

Canna raced to the middle of the river and sank under its waves.

Gentry sighed. Wilma Swansworth was leaving the house. Her eyes glared, and her mouth scowled.

Her hands clenched in fists.

The girl stayed hidden until the danger had passed, then tossed a rock into the middle of the river to signal Canna. The coast was clear. Canna put her head up, but left her body submerged. The dragon asked, "What was it? Who am I hiding from?"

"Wilma Swansworth. We have another matter to bring before the Creator."

Canna sniffed. "That one. Yes, we will pray for her. And about her."

Gentry shook her head. "I guess she hasn't given up on my marrying Brody."

"She is persistent."

"So am I." Gentry smiled a straight-lipped smile.

Canna laughed. "Go home, little one. Call me when your parents say we can meet again for another trip. Or if you need a quick getaway from the Swansworths. I'll be here."

Gentry reached out and hugged Canna's neck one more time. "I will see you again, Canna."

"Yes, you will." Canna flapped her wings and disappeared into the sky.

VOCABULARY LIST

Banished —	Sent away and unable to
return

Breeches —-	Pants

Cascading —-	Falling

Cauldron —-	Large round pot

Crooning —-	Singing softly

Crystalline —-	Like a crystal, a shiny
stone

Decreed —-	Ordered

Deftly —-	Skillfully

Detestable —-	Horrible

Disconcerting —	Bothersome, scary

Disembarked —-	Got down off

Embarrassment —-	Feeling ashamed,
uncomfortable

Emphatic —-	With great energy

Encounter —	Meet

Enraged —-	Angry

Exchange —-	Give one for another

Exhilarating —-	Exciting

Exiled —-	Sent away and unable to return

Fillets —-	Strips of meat or fish

Flanks —-	Outside of the back of the leg

Fledglings —-	Like baby birds learning
to fly

Frolicked —-	Dance around

Fumed —-	Argued

Futile —- Useless

Gawked —- Stared with your mouth open in surprise

Glistened —- Shined

Guidance — Advice, direction

Haunches —- Back legs

Honorable —- Honest, trustworthy

Illuminated —- Lit up with lights

Inedible —- Unable to be eaten

Kaleidoscope —- Colors that look like they are changing all the time

Lore —- Stories

Lowing — Mooing

Luminescent — Shining brightly

Luscious —- Delicious

Magnificent —- Great

Maneuvering —- Moving around

Maturity —- Good sense

Meander —- To weave along, not go in a straight line

Mercantile —- Shop, store

Mottled —- Covered in dark marks

Pearlescent — Sparkling

Plummeted —- Fell from a great height

Prism —- Cut glass that reflects light like a rainbow

Provisions —- Supplies

Renegade —- Someone who turns against a friend

Rummage —- Dig through

Seethed —- Said with anger, through clenched teeth

Severely —-   Seriously

Screeched —-   Screamed

Somber —-   Serious

Talon, Taloned —-Claws, having claws

Treacherous —-   Dangerous

Vapor —-   Fog

Vehemently —-   Strongly

Withered —-   Wrinkled

Writhing —-   Wiggling

ABOUT THE AUTHOR

Colleen K. Snyder has always had a passion for writing. She authored two previously published books: *Journey to Amanah: The Beginning* and *Return to Tebel-Ayr: The Journey Continues* (B&H Publishing). She lives on a "ranchette" in California and is the juniorest ranch hand. She serves on her church prayer team, writes the weekly prayer letter, facilitates a women's Bible Study, and exercises a ministry of intercessory prayer. She has worked as a factory line worker, pharmacy technician, USAF missile systems analyst, janitor, nanny, teacher, accounting manager and anything else the Lord required. Her son, Bear and his wife Krystal, their two daughters, Mara and Kaylynn, and her daughter Katie all live in Ohio.

Colleen's story is for His glory, always.

Connect with her on Facebook at Colleen K. Snyder, Author and on her website colleensnyderauthor.com.